DIRTY GIRL

(Laura laughs)

RM Paul

ISBN: 1795635169
ISBN-13: 978 1795635165

imagine if

1.

The dark clouds hanging overhead at last promised to clear. They were helped on their way by a sudden slam of the plate glass doors closing behind her. Laura stepped out of the job centre, underneath a leaden sky and into the pouring rain.

Whilst litter collectors hid out in greasy spoons and bookmaker shops, used paper cups fought running battles with empty crisp packets. Discarded carrier bags inflated with air and full of opportunity danced with the wind. It was an afternoon to make squirrels and pigeons look exotic and photographers who exposed moody black-and-white shots would be gifted opportunities to win prizes.
Just a typical July afternoon in England.

If Pauline could see what was going through Laura's head, she'd be impressed. To tell her, she'd first have to find her hiding place.

The young lad who'd held the door open asked if she was going to be alright, and Laura didn't mind when he'd finished his sentence with the word 'sweetheart'. She knew *that* word and others like it might annoy some women, but not her. When pressing down onto the curved handle of her wooden walking cane to support her slender frame she noticed it had worn down to a smooth and shiny finish. Edging side-on she raised a hand to signal her appreciation and assure the lad she'd be fine, and it was only then she saw his friend too. They both wore tracksuits, one of them red and the other blue. Neither of these two lads looked athletic in any way but their tops were at least waterproof. Laura had no interest in football.

Taking a long drag on his hand-rolled cigarette before passing it on to his returning mate, the smile from the lad in blue demonstrated how good it was to share. How sweet it smelled as a gust of wind brought second-hand remnants of it Laura's way. Recent memories of a failed attempt to acquire cannabis on prescription from her GP (for medicinal purposes) brought with them a smile. Her smile didn't last long - the wind that whipped through the trees replaced the smell of weed with fresh dogshit. A staffie-cross. She wasn't an expert in the field of animal excrement, but it was the law of averages - right? Whilst her GP hadn't been sympathetic to her actual needs and wants Laura refused his kind offer of the class C and habit-forming Diazepam. But hey, if you don't ask you don't get.

The track-suited lads puffed away whilst settled underneath a 'no smoking' sign, they were proper hard-core alright. 'I'll be finished with my interview in half-an-hour if you fancy hanging around?' one of the lads shouted. 'We could have a bit of fun when I'm finished. You know, if you're up for it?'

'Aw bless. A pity shag.'

Raising her free hand up behind her whilst fighting the temptation to use individual fingers, Laura signalled back that she wouldn't be accepting his generous offer. The mothers of these fine fellas could be proud of the way they'd raised them as they clearly held no prejudice against disabled women. Whilst these lads could only have been seventeen or eighteen-years old, Laura, in her current state looked every day of her age. If only she could thank the boy's mothers for their community spirit.

After tugging on the frayed collar of her tatty old blouse Laura's fingers ran through the greasy blonde hair matted onto her head. To call it dirty blonde wouldn't be a stretch. Fighting to maintain her balance as her dry heaving threatened to topple her sideways, she pictured the two lads running to her rescue if she were to fall over. Experience told her they'd cop a free grope as they helped her up and off the ground. She'd be taxed!

Her turquoise woollen coat was of little use in the rain and there was no point buttoning it up, perhaps it would have fit better had it been bought new from a store. In any event, regardless where she'd bought it, everything she wore was always that annoying half-size out. She wondered where all those pretty girls with the perfectly fitting clothes shopped.

'Or all three of us together.' A counter offer from one of the two lads brought a hearty cackle from his mate. You had to hand it to them, teamwork does make the dream work. The ganja they shared was working its magic.

Slowly edging forward whilst relying on her walking cane for any semblance of balance, with every deliberate step Laura's feet scraped lazily along and against a top layer of gravel chips. Nobody else would give a second thought to those crunchy grating noises below but Laura likened it to a pneumatic drill, or that car alarm that goes off at four o'clock in the morning. Every fucking morning.

From the corner of her eye Laura caught sight of her best friend manically urging her to hurry-up, although she'd parked-up far enough away for it to be a proper chore to get there. Perched forward in her seat and leaning on the steering wheel Pauline was eager to get the hell out of dodge. Some people really should know better, and Pauline knew better than anyone how difficult it was for Laura to have to walk as she did whilst here. To combine this with such levels of concentration, well, it was a job in itself.

Scowling when a momentary lack of focus caused her to stumble over her own clumsy feet Laura figured she was probably still being spied on. To fall over now would certainly be a great show for anyone watching, but she couldn't be bothered with the hassle today. Besides, the ground was soaking wet - and those two lads. Resisting any and all Pauline's efforts to hurry her Laura whispered a different rude word with each cautious step she took. Consequently, it was a good five minutes before she made it to the waiting car - and her despairing friend.

'You could have driven over and got me at the bloody front door.' After throwing her walking cane through the open passenger side window and onto the back seat, to go into attack would be Laura's best line of defence. Shuddering as she reeled off numerous reasons why she couldn't and wouldn't drive to the front entrance Pauline fidgeted back and forth in her seat. She wanted to see if anything of note was happening behind Laura. Try as she might though she couldn't see a thing as Laura was quite annoyingly blocking any and all views of the job centre.

'Is that why you're wearing these things?' laughed Laura, when thrusting her head through the open window. She prodded and pointed at Pauline's oversized designer sunglasses. 'You're more paranoid than me. Are you in disguise? You look like a getaway driver.'

Blushing as she shifted her shades from her eyes and onto the top of her head, Pauline swore as she scrunched up several Greggs the bakers paper bags to stuff them into an already overflowing glove compartment. Rogue sausage-roll and steak bake crumbs were next to feel her wrath when she swiped them off the passenger

seat and down onto the floor. Swearing again w...
stubborn flakes of pastry teased by dancing arou...
fingers she eventually gave up. When urging Laura to g...
out of the rain and into the bloody car, Pauline ordered
her to shift her arse.

'I may have gotten some new material in there,'
said Laura, as with a deal of effort and very little grace she
huffed and puffed to haul herself into the passenger seat.
When winning the fight to free her seatbelt strap to fasten
herself in for blast-off she then continued. 'The woman
started waffling on about the benefits of a regular clock-in
and clock-out.'

Pauline wasn't paying attention.

'Unwitting agents for this government's policy of
genocide by stealth against the working-class.' A change of
tact with some fancy words thrown in to impress was
deployed, and still, none of it was picked up on. As soon as
Laura had settled into her seat the wheels had been set in
motion, literally. They were out of the carpark onto the
main road and into third gear before Laura had even
noticed. A finger or two poked into her friends ribs was
usually what was called for in situations like this. 'You're
not paying attention,' shouted Laura.

Delighted to have put her foot down to get them
out of there safely, Pauline had no idea why she'd been
assaulted. After giving out a yelp and recoiling in fright she
watched Laura sit back and puff out her cheeks. She did
then chuckle too, 'clock-in and clock-out. That's funny.'
She had been listening, better late than never!

After removing her nose from one of her armpits to
bury it into the other, Laura then raised her head again
with a start. Exhaling sharply from her mouth she then
inhaled again slowly, through her nostrils. Those four yoga
classes hadn't been a waste of money after all. Undoing

.ons before digging her nails into her collar
er blouse to draw in another breath. With
t watering she re-emerged from her blouse
y shit.'

Pauline showing little to no interest in
was saying or doing Laura used more force
cessary to adjust her seat. After slamming it
into reve... to allow her enough space to lift her feet up
onto the dashboard she slumped down to tease strands of
her hair through one finger and a thumb of each hand. To
be hidden underneath a wet and greasy cloak was a quiet
and lonely place though. In need of a hug or some
comforting words, if she had to ask for them, she would.
'You haven't been listening to a word I've said you bitch,'
she shouted when raising her head.

Still slightly anxious though undoubtedly highly
focussed, Pauline had reinstated her sunglasses down and
onto her face again. She looked like a formula one racing
car driver from the nineteen-seventies (had women been
allowed to drive them). Sporting her favourite brown
neckerchief scarf that so complimented those tortoiseshell
sunglasses and her pixie-cut jet-black hair, she also looked
like a movie star. Imagining them to be in a convertible car
with the top down, Laura tried but couldn't remember the
name of *that* film. In any boys book Pauline would be a
solid seven or eight out of ten every day of the week.
However, if anyone would ever be so crass to ask Laura to
score her, she'd have no hesitation in giving out a ten. Part
of Pauline's beauty was she didn't have to try too hard.
She could get dressed in the dark and still be amazing.
Today she looked like – Laura couldn't remember her
name, perhaps Laura should cut back on the number of old
movies she liked to watch.

She hadn't had much luck or experience with men though, and Pauline wasn't particularly comfortable talking about that kind of thing with anyone other than Laura. They'd been besties since their primary school days more than twenty years since. Until just a couple of years ago, whenever anything even remotely to do with sex had come up in conversation Pauline had always referred to it as *'the dirty deed'*. One day, and it was completely out of the blue, she'd called it instead just *'the deed'*. For whatever reason, overnight, the dirty had disappeared without trace.

Sooner or later someone would fall madly in love with Pauline and he'd be the luckiest man in the world. If only he'd move his arse and find the courage to talk to and get to know her.

'Audrey Hepburn,' started Laura suddenly. 'Have you seen Breakfast at Tiffany's? We have to watch it when we get home.' Tapping an index finger against her nodding head Laura indicated that a memory was being stored away to be recycled later. It wasn't the film with the two women in the convertible car, but it was a good one. On noting the curious looks she was now receiving, Laura didn't care. She'd at last gotten her friends attention so bemoaned again how badly she smelled and the hideous state of her raggedy clothes. Elevating her sunglasses slowly and just enough to peer beneath them, Pauline leered at her best mate sitting with her feet up on the dashboard. She watched her scratch at her head as if attacking a colony of squatting nits, before she then went on to wrap her arms around herself. She looked to be in dire need of some warm and comforting words.

'Yeah, you're an absolute midden. So what?'

Turning around with such force it felt as if the car had been travelling too fast going over a speed bump,

Laura let out a shrill cry before asking, 'do you think I'm over-doing it?'

'Do you want me to cry? To feel sorry for you,' asked Pauline. Removing one of her hands from the steering wheel to make a clenched fist she turned it against her temple whilst furrowing her brow. 'Oh I'm so sad. Poor me.'

When repositioning her hands onto the steering wheel with an exaggerated thump, Pauline threw a glance of indifference Laura's way. She mixed it with some words of advice too. 'You know what you have to do, and you're good at it. A real pro.' She stopped to wipe some saliva from her bottom lip. 'A pro,' she repeated, before relinquishing to let out a laugh. 'Oh come on. That's not the first time you've been called a pro, is it?'

Turning her knees and shifting her bum before sinking her chin into the palm of her hand, Laura turned away from Pauline with a huff. She didn't have to listen to these insults, there were far more interesting things to be doing.

Tree. Tree. Car. Tree. Car.

A less than perfect view of England's suburban backwaters through the pouring rain wasn't much cope. And wiping clear her misted up window clarified nothing, so when Pauline sniggered before speaking again, she had Laura's full attention. 'Do you remember a couple of years back, the weekend we went down to Glastonbury?'

Laura's smile as she turned again to face Pauline confirmed she did remember. That weekend was the first time they'd been to a music festival together, and the first time either of them had been camping. It had furnished them both with several great new memories to sit alongside the so many others they'd already shared.

'Yeah, well. Do you remember when you ambushed me on the last day? With your sleeping bag. You jumped on me from behind to cocoon me in it for at least five minutes.'

'I do,' laughed Laura. 'Three nights I slept in that thing. Fully clothed, for the most part. Yeah, it must have stank. Sorry.'

'It wasn't you sleeping in it that freaked me out. It was the thought of all the farting and the shagging you'd been doing in it, that's what gave me the bile.'

'Ha-ha. I forgot all about that. That was one of my favourite weekends ever. We should definitely do that again sometime.'

'I did enjoy the music.'

Pauline's mind drifted back to her best memories of that weekend too. As a music lover that trip had been her idea and she'd seen some great new bands as well as loads of her old favourites.

'Anyway, stop getting off the bloody subject. How you look and smell now isn't too different to when we left Glasto that day. And these days, you have to do what you have to do.' Taking hold of Laura's coat to shake it back-and-forth, Pauline went on. 'This, these,' she said, when letting go of the coat to highlight everything Laura was wearing. 'These rags. Your unwashed hair and no make-up. This, this is your uniform. You know that, so get over it.'

Pauline mock scowled theatrically to smell the fingers she'd used to hold Laura's minging jacket. Laura's smile was a blend of courteous and apologetic and confirmed that no more need be said. The sooner Pauline got them back to her mother's house to allow Laura the time and space for a good wash and a change of clothes, the better for all concerned.

'I'm going to need a right good scrub this time. This is the mankiest I've been for one of those meetings. I'd bet diamonds that if we went directly to the airport, they wouldn't let me on the plane.'

A nod of her head was all Pauline said. She needn't bring up the rank rotten smell again.

Switching on the car stereo introduced the sound of an old Brit-pop classic that brought with it a glistening smile to re-illuminate Laura's pretty face. Enthusiastically nodding her head in time with the beat of the song, everything in Laura's world was suddenly in tune again. With her feet still settled on top of the dashboard she used her hands to tap out a beat onto her thighs.

'I didn't take that sleeping bag home,' confessed Laura, as her mind drifted back alongside the music. 'I put it in a bin, before we left Glastonbury.'

'I know, I was there. It was such a waste though. You should have given it to a homeless person, it could have helped to keep them warm for a while.'

'I never thought about that. I mean, no offence and all but they probably wouldn't have minded sleeping with that putrid smell.'

'Sleep in it!' Pauline spat out a laugh. 'Fuck-off. When they put a match to it and set it on fire, that's what would have kept them warm. It was proper revolting, even for them.'

As their laughter softened Laura leant across to lay her head gently onto her best friends shoulder. Whilst Pauline kept her eyes fixed on the road ahead, visible in the rear-view mirror her smile emanated down. Travelling swiftly along a desolate road in even more desperate weather it was warm and cosy where they were, together. As the song playing was about to hit its high point, Laura lifted her head from Pauline's shoulder to sit up and lean forward. After turning down the volume of the now redundant heating fans she turned up the volume on the radio.

'Dirty girl,' Pauline shouted with a smile, as she joined Laura in readying herself for the chorus.

At the top of their voices, and in perfect harmony, they all sang along.

'ALL THE PEOPLE - SO MANY PEOPLE.'

2

Binmen were picking along the sand in competition with screeching scavenging seabirds and they all chased behind the beep-beep-beeping refuse truck on an otherwise peaceful promenade. The frisky sun had yet to catch fire, permitting absent-minded visitors more time to apply their factor thirty. The forecast for today was the same as yesterdays, and there'd be no change tomorrow. Scorchio.

At the far end of the beach was a party of five who'd been camped there since the previous afternoon. Whilst four of them were stretched-out and fast asleep, the other, his name was Sebastian (probably), strummed on an acoustic guitar. Three girls and two boys it was. The other bloke, Barnaby (probably), had at last made good use of his tom-tom drums by utilising them as a makeshift pillow. The steady rhythm of his heartbeat was palpably more agreeable to one of the young ladies than his virtuoso musicianship had been. With her head resting on his chest, Tabatha (probably) lay by his side.

Annaliese and Jemima (probably) slept solo, they would have other days. With jobs in public-relations and journalism waiting for them they'd be introduced to men in positions of power and authority who would sweep them off their feet. It was the perfect career choice for these young women to fulfil their long-held ambitions. Codenamed networking, within a few years they'd be discontented mothers and financially sound but destitute housewives. They'd care for their pedigree dog (neutered), have two cars, two-point-two children and vacation three times annually. Daddy's initial disappointment in their inability to bag a handsome Prince at their prestigious universities would be forgotten. The substantial financial outlay he'd shelled out on his Princess's education would eventually pay a handsome dividend; regardless how ungrateful she always remains.

If they hadn't parted ways with some of their allowances to their latest on-trend causes of Amnesty International and Greenpeace (to ease their conscience's), all five of them could have gone to Goa for the summer. That aside, Annaliese is a nervous flyer and no amount of medication could help, neither was there enough room in the hold for the number of sick bags required. Jemima is afraid of needles and the vaccinations required, the MeToo tattoo just above her navel (although pretty) was henna and only temporary. It's the thought that counts.

If any of them needed a hug, mummy and daddy were only a short aeroplane trip away. Additionally, if any common riff-raff holidaymakers were to somehow get a hold of their plastic, causing them to run short on cash, they could draw lots to see which of them would contact home to have more money sent over. Paying back such loans wouldn't be an issue as they'd been very adept at keeping hold of all receipts to claim back as allowable expenses. Best of all though, in choosing this somewhat whimsical location for their annual soiree, collectively their Insta and Twitter numbers had gone through the roof. #Super.

'Middle-class wankers.' observed the well-tanned one of three lads who stood watching from the promenade. Wearing a Ramones t-shirt he wasn't much into acoustic guitars. 'Let's go in here,' he continued, when pointing toward a little café signposted as LP's place. Homemade and distinctive, the cafes sign had been assembled by attaching several timeworn vinyl records onto a wooden board.

Anyone worth their salt knows the first thing you need to do on a Spanish holiday island (after dropping of your luggage) is find the best place for a good breakfast. Full English and fried, obviously.

Having walked the length of the promenade on this their preliminary scouting mission there'd been no real thought behind the lads choosing this café. Their aching feet and growling tummies might have pushed them in that direction anyway, but an enticing racket gathered them in.

'Girl fight. And it sounds like a couple of lezzers,' said the tanned lad as he rubbed his hands in anticipation. Striding into the courtyard of the cafe like a man on a mission (in case anyone was watching) he took his seat at what he presumed to be the head of the table. There were eight tables to choose from, each of them charming and round with freshly painted white wooden slats. Each table offered a choice of four chairs in a range of different colours. The tanned lad took his place in the black chair.

'Lezzers! Was that aeroplane a time machine and we've been transported back to the eighties? I wouldn't mind the music, but the company I'm keeping could use an upgrade. I mean, lezzers. Really?' one of the other lads remarked as he sat down in a yellow chair. The pink chair was cast-adrift without a second thought.

'Rug-munchers then. You know what I mean.'

'And now we're back in the seventies,' scoffed the other of the three lads.

Ridiculing laughter from the tanned lads two mates was shelved when the thunderous noise of stainless-steel implements being thrown across a tiled kitchen floor was accompanied by a shriek. That racket was quickly followed by the appearance of a young woman standing in the open doorway of the café. After glancing first to confirm she had customers, she then took a pencil from her left pocket and a paper pad from the one opposite.

Liam used his sweaty palms to push down discreetly onto the armrests of his chair, he'd felt himself sliding down into it causing him to quietly bemoan his poor posture. The tub-thumping drums of a melodramatic backing track wasn't in harmony with the woman now making her way to his table. Her blonde hair caught the sun rising behind and caused an aurora to beam on and off like a searchlight. With her head tilting gently from side-to-side as she strode forward confidently and yet seemingly in slow-motion toward him, Liam assumed the background music was a sure-fire warning that something major was about to happen. Foreseeing the building behind being engulfed in flames, the backdraft of a mushroom cloud explosion would catch hold of her clothing and she'd be thrown into his outstretched and open arms. He wondered if his two mates could hear the same music.

Whilst undoubtedly attractive, the woman had an almost colourless face that was in stark contrast to her mesmerising green eyes. The shape of her smile enhanced with each step she took.

'Good morning lads,' she beamed with an electricity that outshone the sun set free behind her. 'My names Laura, what can I do for you?'

'Can you dance naked in a cage?' came the reply from the lad in the black chair.

When introducing herself Laura's arms were already raised to show a little pad in her right hand and a pencil in her left. She was left-handed, but Liam didn't believe in any of that witchcraft hocus-pocus crap. Although unable to fully comprehend what had just happened, he was doubtful now that the building behind was going to explode in dramatic circumstances. He ought really to stop watching those Tarantino movies. The one thing Liam didn't doubt - his mate was a fucking tool.

'Alright Sammy Davis, calm down.'

Recoiling her neck, slanting her head and squinting her eyes simultaneously to get a better look at who or what was sitting in front of her, Laura wondered why she'd plumped for Sammy Davis. This idiot was more orange than brown or black. Unsure at first if she'd been rumbled by the guy sitting in the yellow chair to her left, or if he was just illiterate to Hollywood legends, Laura scowled when he had the audacity to query, 'Sammy Davis?'

'Junior. Sammy Davis junior,' said Liam, with a glint in his eye and a knowing grin. 'He was a singer and an actor. And a black man. Sammy Davis Junior I mean.'

'Is that not racist?'

Following the second stupid question in quick succession from the guy in the yellow chair, Laura figured she'd gotten away with one. She at the same time tried to remember the names of munchkins from the chocolate factory movies, although he probably wouldn't have gotten that reference either. Maybe he wasn't the sharpest tool in the shed.

'Enlighten me Casper,' replied Laura. 'As in Casper the friendly ghost.' She elaborated her point, as he clearly needed some help. Drumming her pencil up and down onto her pad she glanced to her right to see if the guy in the red chair had caught onto that reference too. Mildly amused as he sat back languidly to cross his legs and make himself at home, Liam's demeanour was non-committal. With no response from any of the three lads Laura stopped her drumming. Surveying the silence she wondered which of them would be the first to speak-up and order something. The guy in the black chair straight ahead, the one she'd referred to as Sammy Davis, well he was deep in thought. Looking into his empty eyes Laura assumed there was nothing much behind them either. He was so stupid he was probably thinking about-

'The thing is, I'm not stupid.'

The tanned lads blinking eyes seemed to force open his mouth and he began to plead his case. He explained his thought process of taking a three-week course of sunbed sessions before coming out on holiday. What his brief diatribe lacked in full disclosure or honesty, it made up for in drama.

The truth of it was, on his very first visit to the sunbed salon he'd taken a bit of a shine to the lady who worked the front desk. She had a great tan herself (a perk of the job no doubt) and the tight tunic she wore presented her tits very favourably. He was aware, as most men are, that the primary function of tits are to feed babies. However, like all men, he was immature and just wanted to play with them. A name badge pinned onto her uniform said her name was Susie and she'd made him feel very welcome. It was only a matter of time before she'd unlock his booth from the outside to step in and suck him off. Surely?

Another thing he failed to mention was, if anyone were to have a close look at the results of these sunbed sessions, they'd see he had what could pass as a natural tan, because of his tan lines. This was more down to good fortune rather than any advanced planning though. For his first two weeks of sessions he hadn't removed his boxers (if Susie were to come in, she would surely improvise). He'd barely spoken a word to Susie the whole time he'd been going there and as such had been too afraid to ask about the potential risks of the dreaded ball cancer. She would've been biased in any answer she'd have given anyway, so there was no real point talking to her. He'd spent his final week of sessions dancing naked holding onto the handrails above and Susie never did enter his booth, but that was probably because the shop was busy most of the time. Probably.

'So, whilst these morons are hiding out in the shade, I'll be on the beach. Neck-deep in clunge.'

He couldn't help himself.

'You don't get out much do you?' replied Laura. She didn't miss a beat when doing so and managed to be heard over the exasperated groans of the tanned lads two friends. When she finished with a shout of, 'shamone motherfucker,' she'd resisted the temptation to give out a high-pitched 'woo-hoo', or to moonwalk. She didn't want to make it too easy for them. Internally cursing that munchkins weren't individually named, she decided to stick with her 'black' theme.

'Michael Jackson,' howled Liam. He laughed so hard he almost fell backwards. 'Brilliant.' In the excitement of saving himself from falling over he'd also spat out a little saliva. Fortunately, with all eyes elsewhere he was sure Laura the waitress hadn't noticed anything untoward. He was joined in his hilarity by his friend in the yellow chair opposite, Casper.

'So, you think you're a comedian?' The tanned lads overtly sarcastic tone should have been a clue that it was a rhetorical question. However, as it was also asked with a hint of acrimony it demanded an answer.

'You're not so stupid after all,' replied Laura. 'You can catch my act at Yosser's place, if you fancy a decent night out.' The words danced from her lips.

More certain than ever he was being made a fool of, and receiving no help from his mates, the disgruntled lad with the tan demanded to speak with the manager or the cafes owner. Finishing his rant on a high by deriding her general attitude he was going to show her, or at least have her gaffer do it for him. And if he were to do that in public, then all the better.

'Him! Really?' Laura scoffed, before continuing with displeasure paired with an unchaperoned indignation specifically designed to belittle the recipient. 'You're speaking to her. Well, fifty-percent of her. The other fifty-percent is in the kitchen. I can fetch her out too if you like. I should warn you though, she's pretty pissed off right now. Oh – And by the way.' Laura paused to dampen a finger and thumb to wipe at some stains on her white blouse, before continuing, 'the soups off,' she chuckled heartily, as though she'd belatedly gotten the punchline to a joke she'd been told much earlier.

'It's okay. We don't need to be speaking with any of the other owners,' consoled Liam, whilst waving his hands around in a light-hearted and friendly manner. The whole show had become a little ridiculous, particularly from his mate who was being a bit of a dick. There'd been two late call-offs from this holiday, Mark and Gareth. The thing was, Liam couldn't really blame them as he'd contemplated doing the same thing himself. It had been proposed during numerous conversations that this trip could turn out to be one huge babysitting job. Ultimately, it was Mark and Gareth who'd won the battle of nerves in leaving it late enough to come up with a phoney yet plausible enough excuse to cancel their holiday. And already, they'd been proven to be correct in doing-so.

Laura thought the guy in the red chair seemed okay. He had nice teeth that encouraged you to look up into his brown eyes before then being drawn to his swept across though casually ungroomed dark hair. He wore a casual white shirt with its sleeves rolled halfway up his lower arm. The top two buttons were undone and if he were to throw a loosened necktie around the collar, he'd be a dead-ringer for a young Bryan Ferry. On their quieter days Laura and Pauline would amuse themselves by suggesting why customers were so exacting in the colour of chair they chose. In this instance, Laura saw red for danger.

'I'm sorry. What?'

Liam's broadening smile suggested he didn't mind that Laura hadn't taken in much of what he'd said, which had included a wholehearted apology for his errant friend. He repeated most of it again, only this time he'd also conclude with some formal introductions. 'Having gotten past all of that I propose we start afresh. Laura, it's nice to meet you. My name's Liam. Sitting directly across from me is my good friend Graeme.' Laura nodded her head in appreciation of Liam's fine manners before then turning to her left to give a similar nod to Casp- not Casper, Graeme, who from his sedentary position in the yellow chair offered a friendly though slightly nervous wave. 'And Laura, this goofy young chap is- '

'Irrelevant,' announced Laura, who without any warning decided she'd heard quite enough. 'I'll bring you out three breakfasts, full English. I'll also bring you a pot of tea and a pot of coffee, you can fight over who gets what.' Turning on her heels and her toes Laura strutted off without saying another word. Whilst resisting the temptation to look around, from an ever-increasing distance she could hear two of the lads beginning to debate amongst themselves. The other one was smiling.

Busily mopping up a puddle of carrot and coriander soup, Pauline offered an apology as soon as Laura came striding into the kitchen. She'd already picked up from the floor the large ladle and cooking pot that only a few minutes earlier she'd hurled in Laura's general direction. There was never any danger of it hitting Laura, and she'd barely flinched when it had whizzed past her.

'You know I like to come into a tidy shop in the morning,' remarked Pauline. 'And it was your turn.'

'I know, and I'm sorry too. I promise It won't happen again.'

'That's what you said the last time.' Spots of green and orange liquid splashed against the stainless-steel legs of worktops, as like a Kendo sword Pauline flashed back and forth the handle of her mop.

At the end of business each day and on closing the café, Laura and Pauline would take turns each for just one of them to stay behind. That person would then do most of the cleaning and wiping down of surfaces, the putting away of any unused ingredients, cutlery and tableware. All the mundane stuff punters never have to think about or see. On walking to work this very morning Laura had remembered and thought it best to admit she might have forgotten to do a full clean and tidy-up, which may have included not putting away a pot half-full of soup.

The thing that pissed off Pauline most wasn't that Laura had just had a flaky 'blonde' moment and forgotten to do as she should, she'd owned up to neglecting her duties because she'd taken a guy into the back of the café again. And she didn't mean bringing the same man back to the café again and again, she meant a new man. It was another man, Laura was a recidivist. Some guy had popped in for a cup of coffee and within ten minutes of him sitting down she'd organised an illicit tryst between them.

As well as apologising, Laura had tried to justify what happened by emphasising how handsome this guy had been. Pauline held counsel on that point but thought she'd seen the fella in question. On leaving the café she'd noticed a creepy looking character hanging around looking suspicious. She'd even readied her mobile phone to call the local police - or smash him in the face with it, whichever would have been easier at the time. Pauline better understood now why he'd been acting like a weirdo. He'd been instructed by Laura to stay hidden until the coast was clear - but hiding behind a tree hadn't been a good look for him. On top of everything else Pauline remembered he was a little too hairy for her liking, and with his flimsy goatee beard he looked like a runty little forest creature. Long story short Pauline thought he was ugly as sin. He wasn't even Laura's usual type, as in she didn't go for the poncey bohemians. But they do say a change is as good as a rest, and Laura didn't take many rests.

'What did you say to get this one to come back?'

Laura turned away from Pauline and toward the fridge, but not before a guilty smile and a telling hint of blush had been set free.

'Oh no! You didn't, did you? You bloody did. Again!'

Further interrogation only caused Laura to take longer than was necessary to get a few simple ingredients out of the fridge. She also made a point of singing out loud the names of each of the things she was searching for, 'mushrooms…… Eggs………. Sausages…… and - What?' With a handful of ingredients and a headful of mischief Laura turned again to face Pauline, and the music. Holding her nerve and her tongue for as long as she could, Laura tried to play dumb. Unfortunately for her, Pauline could read the signs and knew Laura was anything but dumb.

'He came here for a cup of coffee, and you told him you wanted to sit on his face.'

The slanting of Laura's head and the raising of her arms and hands was the giveaway a guilty plea was on its way. 'He asked me what I recommended,' she chortled. She then laughed some more, partly through a relief that the truth was out, but also because she'd managed to save three eggs from falling onto the floor to join the spots of soup. 'What did you expect me to say?'

'Well, seeing how this is a café. A cappa-fucking-cino would've been a decent start,' said Pauline, as she couldn't help but laugh too. 'Oh, I'm only jealous,' she went on to concede, when resting her chin down onto the top of her mop handle. 'It's been that long since I did *the deed*. I swear, I think it's almost healed up.' Removing a hand from her mop, Pauline pointed somewhat awkwardly in the general direction of her genitalia.

After placing the eggs down to take hold of Pauline's hand into her own, Laura said she needed to show her something. Leading her out of the kitchen to peer through a window looking onto the tables in the courtyard, she pointed to the three guys sat there.

'The guy sitting in the yellow chair, he seems like a nice fella.' Pauline nodded her head. She liked his New Order t-shirt and trusted her friend's judgement. He was also handsome, to a point. 'However,' came Laura's warning. 'The problem with that guy. Well, he's a touch wet behind the ears I think.'

Pointing next, and somewhat extravagantly to the guy sitting in the red chair Laura began again. 'That one. Now, on first impressions. I don't know. He seems interesting, but he's probably in the same boat as his mate in the yellow chair. As in they're both a bit slow.'

Noting the curious glances from Pauline, Laura knew she'd have to elaborate. She began with a sigh, 'the point being,' she carried on with zeal. 'The chances of either of those two asking you out on a date for a drink - and let's not beat around the bush here, a shag-'

Apologising for her unintended double-entendre, it was only after Pauline had stopped her sniggering and repeatedly saying the word 'bush' in a mock French accent that Laura caught-on to what she'd said. Laura stood upright and brought Pauline with her. 'Now this one.' An accusing finger jabbed straight ahead to the tanned guy in the black chair.

'Donald Trump,' shouted Pauline, before throwing a hand over her mouth to suggest an apology. She couldn't help herself, she'd been caught up in the theatre of Laura's performance.

'Genius,' laughed Laura. 'Donald Trump. Why didn't I think of him? I went down the black route, and he's so obviously orange.'

'Did you ask him to name two Ramones songs?' asked Pauline.

'No, I didn't.'

'You usually do.'

'I know, and they never can.'

Laura shushed Pauline to explain how that guy was different from the other two, and not in a good way. She told how, of the three, he would be their leader. He was their show-off and so-called alpha. Of the three he would be the one that ended up with the girl at the end of the night. Laura explained that his type was so full of crap and not afraid to share it they could front up and talk to girls about any old shit. And sometimes it didn't even matter what these guys said. Depending on the circumstances it could be something as lurid as 'nice tits doll'. Laura grabbed hold of her chest as she said this. She also screwed up her face to put on a mock Cockney accent for added effect (It was a north south divide thing). 'They can and will talk to twenty different girls on any given night and they'll ask ten of those girls out. It doesn't matter to them how many knock-backs they get as they have no shame. But when they do get a yes, then it's a result. For him and his type it's a numbers game. Nothing more, nothing less.'

'Look, look,' the tanned lad shouted. Jumping up and out of his black chair he pointed to the cafes window. 'She wants me. I fucking knew it.'

'I'm almost too afraid to ask, but okay. Go on.' Liam despaired. Leaning forward and bending down to tie up his shoelaces which were already tied but perhaps needed a little tightening at least hid some of his shame. Whilst he couldn't face looking at his mate, he didn't want to be caught looking toward the café either. He didn't know where to look.

'Are you blind? Didn't you see her looking at me as she played with her little titties? And she was making a face like she was having an orgasm.'

'Honestly, have you ever been with a woman? A real woman,' asked Liam, with an anguished shake of his head. Graeme laughed when Liam then added that family members don't count. It wasn't as if their dick of a mate didn't deserve it.

Graeme's head darted back and forth between his idiotic mate and the attractive woman stood next to the waitress who'd taken their orders. Well, sort of taken their orders.

With his head down and subdued, Liam wasn't for listening to his mates imagined list of all the birds he'd shagged. It was an extensive list that included two mum's they knew and Graeme's sister. Neither did he notice his mate peeling off his Ramones t-shirt in slow-motion.

'I'll show her the message has been received and understood. And why not give her a sneak preview of some of the goods too?' After tossing his t-shirt onto the back of his chair he indulged in a choreographed stretch. Rotating first to his left and then to his right he pulled off some oblique twists. Pulling in his belly with his shoulders back and feet apart (like a powerful politician) he was doing some of his finest work. Running his hands through his hair whilst flexing his puny biceps he strutted like a courting pea- '

'Cock.' Liam wasn't impressed. 'I pity the fool,' he continued in a mock American accent. 'Sit down you fucking idiot,' he finished with, in his own dialect.

'Mr T,' laughed Graeme, who couldn't help but look away from the café. So good was Liam's impromptu impersonation he grabbed at the opportunity to join in with the fun, and in turn gain some revenge for his sisters good name. Together they belted out a repetitive chorus of ridiculing, 'I pity the fool' Mr T impersonations. As their friend conceded to sit down silently, Liam and Graeme roared with laughter.

'You see what I mean,' groaned Laura. 'Look at them horsing around. Honestly, I wish I could say the circus has just pulled into town. Only, how many fucking circuses are there? And why do they always end up here? And guess which one's leading the way? The idiot's taken off his top to show us his moobs. And look how hilarious those two think he is, look how they laugh.'

'He probably farted. Out loud I mean,' added Pauline. 'Boys always think that's funny.'

'I don't mean to nag.'

Turning away from the window and her view of the three lads alacrity, Pauline took a seat to face Laura.

Whilst feigning displeasure at what she figured was going to be a lecture or another life lesson, the truth was she didn't mind listening to these. When it came to men, Laura was very astute and always worth listening to. She was an expert in the field.

'You can,' Laura began in earnest, 'along with most of the women on this planet, hang around and wait for some guy to come and ask you out. The thing is though, most of those guys will be like that clown out there. Granted, sometimes these boys with their locker room talk will be rejected. However, whether it's a case of settling for the least bad option or just being so fucking horny and desperate you end up surrendering, it's these assholes with the bullshit that will - In part supported by us women - eventually go on to father the next generation of asshole misogynists. It is I'm sorry to say a perpetual cycle of bullshit, and in some respect we women are the architects of our own misfortune.'

Laura had clearly given this declaration a lot of prior thought and Pauline had a question or two. However, she'd only managed to spit out the words, 'damn those bloody Spice Girls,' when Laura intimated by holding up her index finger, she'd only been catching her breath. She had more to say on the matter and any questions Pauline had would have to wait.
'Go out and choose a man for yourself. Choose a man for the night the weekend or for life, but don't hang around waiting to be asked. You make the choice. If not for ourselves Pauline, we need to do this for our daughters and our grand-daughters.'

3

A friendly wave to acknowledge the house singer and general compere Dusty, was the first order of business. She was winding up her act with another encore. A nod to Manuel was next. He too was exactly where you'd expect to find him, slouched across the end of the bar. He wasn't much cope as a barman and an average glass-collector too, but he was only young and a likeable lad. Laura leant across and over the bar to shout out a quick hello to Yoz with a question on his general wellbeing. With his back turned he was busily tidying up his cold storage units. They were in no immediate danger of running dry, but they should always be filled to the brim and rotated regularly. Just in case.

'What do you want? I've got no money.' was his terse and utterly predictable reply. He'd recognised the voice but was so busy he hadn't time to do a 180 degree turn in his wheelchair. The sheepish look from Manuel suggested he'd just had a telling off for not sorting out those fridges.

'What are folks on nowadays?' Yoz then asked, without bothering to turn around.

Another glance to Manuel with questioning hands brought only a shrug in reply. The poor lad looked knackered, he should probably go for a siesta to rest his weary shoulders. With her faint smile morphing to a grimace Laura prepared to batten down her hatches after asking Yoz what he was talking about?

'Jesus H Christ.' Raising his arms in the air before lowering one hand onto each of his wheels (a well-practised manoeuvre performed in slow-motion), Yoz spun himself around. His head purposefully sloping to one side whilst his eyes never left yours advertised his disbelief. 'Ching, jellies, shrooms, dexies, eccies, roofies, meth, spice. What is it people are taking nowadays? What are they taking that means they don't need or want to drink any booze? Specifically, my booze?'

Bad-tempered and mean-spirited replies would be the only thing achieved were Yoz to be asked how he knew about those drugs. No questions were asked, as Laura had heard many a fanciful story about rave culture from 'back in the day'. Those were the days, apparently.

'I don't think it has anything to do with drugs.' With an outstretched arm and a fair impersonation of a television weathergirl to highlight tonight's crowd, Laura bemoaned the lack of any punters in the pub who were under the age of forty. It was far nearer fifty, but she kept that to herself. She didn't want to upset Yoz any further.

Utilising his armrests to push himself up and out of his wheelchair to peer over the bar counter, Yoz saw that other than Laura and Manuel he was perhaps the youngest person in tonight. Settling into his chair again he scratched at his chin coated with a grey stubble that was borne from idleness rather than design. 'A license to print money, that's what everyone always says. Fucking liars.' he murmured again his general disapproval.

Having seen and heard it all before Laura didn't pay anymore heed to the continuing grumblings from behind the bar. Her attention had been grabbed by two of the establishments better-known and well-liked locals. Bill and Christina were a couple who'd met when they'd worked for the BBC. Bill had been a cameraman whilst Christina was a professional dancer with a troupe on Top of the Pops. They'd retired to the island more than a decade ago and been regulars in Yoz's bar since. During a party to celebrate their fortieth wedding anniversary (held in honour, in Yosser's), Bill and Christina had been asked to divulge their secrets in maintaining such a long and loving marriage. Without having to think Bill had said it was all about honesty - The ability to be open and honest with each other, always. Christina had laughed when telling everyone you need a bloody good sense of humour. Bill had seen Laura come into the bar and been trying to get her attention since, stood by his table he waved and saluted intermittently. The merry widows, also in their usual seats and in front of Bill scowled their general disapproval. Bill saw them but didn't care, he's always had a real soft spot for Laura and Pauline.

The widows. It was assumed all three of them were widows, although no-one knew for sure because everyone was too afraid to ask. The merry though, now that was a definite misnomer. All three of them had been coming here this same month for the past four years and they were always stony-faced and ghastly serious. Rarely did any of them raise a smile. Perhaps they hadn't quite gotten past the grief stage yet.

'Viagra,' declared Laura, as she gave a nod and a wave to Bill. 'If you have a drug problem in here, it'll be Viagra.'

'Thank-you very much, thank-you.' Dusty the drag artist finished her final encore, although she never did leave the little stage before giving one, it was just her way. Whilst accepting a polite round of applause that would have been more in-tune with a gentle golf stroke, she bowed her head to whisper muted insults about such ungrateful philistines. She had in the past been caught whispering her put-downs when she hadn't bothered to bow, but some of these old bastards are deaf as doorposts and can lip-read. Life is a lesson. Learning, always learning.

Dusty also used her bowing head to glance across and get the nod from Laura.

'And now,' she proclaimed, with a little more intensity to fire up the crowd. 'Ladies and gentlemen, you know the fucking score. No photographs and no filming - For security reasons. Now please everyone, put your hands together and welcome your favourite and my favourite dirty girl – Ladies and gentlemen, It's Laura laughs.'

'Thank-you Dusty. Please, everyone put your hands together to show your love and appreciation for Dusty Springclean.' With her hands clapping above her head Laura led the way to shout out her thanks. This had the effect of bringing about Dusty's best round of applause of the evening. The fact that it was always given as she was leaving the stage wasn't lost on her.

To an almost rapturous welcome Laura was helped up the little step and onto the meagre stage by Dusty's outstretched hand. Leading the applause was Bill, with one foot up on his chair he was bent over to bang his hand down onto his table to simulate a drumroll. Not so overjoyed were the merry widows. One of them tapped gently a solitary finger onto the side of her glass of Gin and Tonic, although it might well have been brim-full of her own tears. At least she was participating to some extent. Her two friends by her side sat almost catatonic, as if auditioning to be extras for the Queen Vic in Albert Square.

'Jesus, hasn't she got great tits?' Watching Dusty's exit after whispering her own personal thank-you, Laura had then pointed to her ample bosom. 'I'm so jealous. And they're all hers.'

'They'd better be. They cost me three fucking grand,' sneered Dusty as she departed. Lifting the hem of her sequined dress she made good her escape toward the gent's toilets. 'Go on, fuck-off you old fool,' she then barked, when slapping the arse of one of the regulars who'd rushed past her to take his seat in time for Laura's show. Such was the old gents flux he was still trying to pull up his zip and fix his belt. 'You never washed your hands you dirty old bastard,' she shouted some more. The number of things Dusty liked to hate had multiplied quite significantly recently, but there was nothing more abhorrent to her than having to hitch up her dress to take a piss in the men's urinals. She was saving up as much money as she could to complete her *transformation,* but it was taking far longer than she'd have liked.

To anyone who hasn't stood on a stage before or given any kind of performance to any crowd, to watch what Laura does looks easy. Taking a moment to look out at the audience and compose her thoughts she blocked out any white noise. Scant twin-spotlights illuminated a haze of second-hand tobacco smoke that lingered to envelope a thousand and one tiny dust particles. And wrapped up within all of this sat a crowd. They were Laura's crowd.

'I might as well be up front with you straight away,' began Laura, with a concerned look that creased her face. Her disposition was at once mirrored by her audience. 'It's so obvious, you're going to notice anyway,' she went on disconsolately. 'I've got a right itchy fanny.'

Some people make it look easy, it's not.

Howls of relief encircled the room hand in hand with laughter. The sight of spilt drinks being wiped from men's shirts and table tops was Laura's cue to turn her back on everyone. With her feet wide-apart and knees akimbo she used the hand that held the microphone to hoist up the front of her skirt. The jutting movement of her right elbow implied she was clawing at something or somewhere furiously. The sound of her frantic scratching and intense orgasmic moaning was amplified by her microphone.

'Fucking hell, I needed that,' said Laura with a 'phew,' as she turned around whilst adjusting her skirt. 'I do also need to say, we've had some complaints recently. About me and my foul language.' Pouting her lips, Laura gave her audience ample time to boo their disapproval. A few of them looked around the room for someone to lynch. 'I know, I know. It's about some of the words I use to describe my.' Pointing vaguely and apologetically at her crotch, she continued with an awkward shape to her mouth. 'You know, down there. Apparently, fan- No, I won't.' Pretending with a wide-open mouth to say the word 'fanny,' but succeeding only in repeatedly exhaling (as if afflicted with an asthma attack) brought more howls of laughter. 'So, this got me thinking. I definitely can't use the C word, obviously. You know cun - Stop it!' An accusing finger pointing around the room brought more laughter. 'So, what are the choices left open to me? Well, there's always 'the lady garden' – Or 'my intimate area'. Well they're both bollocks so I've decided to go with - the vadge. I know, doesn't it sound great – Say it with me, out loud. The vadge.'

With her hand gripped tight onto the front of her skirt Laura formally introduced her vadge to the audience, and vice-versa. Whilst allowing everyone a little time to settle, she took some time out herself to examine closely her fingernails from all angles. 'And look, another thing,' she began again. 'I've got no bloody fingernails either.'

When raising one of her hands up and into the spotlight behind, she allowed everyone to see what she could. 'Now, I know what you're thinking. Never mind the fingernails, get back onto the juicy stuff. Well you're all bloody perverts.'

As laughing men nodded heads, their wives and partners suppressed sniggers. Unspoken orders from the eyes were given but ignored.

'The thing is,' Laura began again. 'These stories are connected. Earlier today I was in the hypermarket, and when I handed over the money for my shopping the guy behind the counter jumped back and stared at me in disgust. When I looked down at my hands to see what he was looking at, well fuck me sideways, I looked like a werewolf. My fingernails were jam-packed full of my pubes, from all the scratching I'd been doing. You know, on my vadge. Now, I'm not going to lie, I did try and bluff it. I winked at the guy and whispered to him all sexily like. Hey, how you doing? Well that didn't work, you men are so fucking fussy nowadays. I blame these dating apps, not to mention we're on an island famed for the availability of casual sex. So, anyway. I had to get the clippers out pronto, didn't I? And I do mean pronto. It cost me four euros and ninety-nine cents for a pair of nail clippers. Daylight fucking robbery.'

With her audience delirious with shock and in fits of laughter through her delivery and impeccable timing, Laura went in for the kill. 'On the plus-side, I might get some of that money back. I went online and I've found a company that buys people's hair. You know, to make wigs. I know, can you fucking imagine? My pubes are going to be sitting on top of an old man's bald head. Stop-it! Behave yourselves.'

Pausing for a breath, Laura allowed everybody to catch there's too.

'Now, I know what you're all thinking,' she began again with a twinkle in her eye. 'A young woman like me, doesn't she shave or wax down there? I believe all the trendy birds are going Brazilian or Hollywood nowadays. You know, down below. On the vadge. Isn't that the truth Christina?' Finishing with a nod and a wink toward Bill and Christina's table was allowed, they were always up for a giggle and some audience participation.

'It's alopecia,' Bill stood up to shout, and he'd cupped his hands around his mouth to make sure everyone could hear him. With his own hands otherwise engaged he found it difficult to deflect the slaps to his thighs and his bum from his loving wife. The expletive that ran free from Laura's mouth wasn't part of her act, she hadn't expected any direct reply to her own punchline. But God love Bill and Christina, you could always rely on them.

Standing alone on the outside patio of Yosser's bar, and unseen by Laura was one of the three guys who'd been in her café earlier that day. It was the guy who'd sat in the red chair, Liam. He was laughing. He laughed because what Laura had told him was true, she was a comedian. But he also laughed because she was funny, very funny. And this crowd was obviously in love with her.

4.

Two claims of minor harassment had been followed by a comical 'almost' karate fight. Those events were then followed by a grand finale of some projectile vomiting onto a busy dancefloor. Liam hadn't seen such a mad rush or heard so much screaming since that latest baby-faced boyband had visited his city. The previous evening, that had threatened to be an unmitigated disaster, had ended on an absolute high when Liam had been set free to saunter around the island. In wandering aimlessly and alone he'd found himself a fair way off the beaten track, and in doing so stumbled upon the old spit and sawdust boozer called Yosser's. Outside that run-down old pub was a beaten-up chalkboard that joyfully promoted, amongst other things, a stand-up comedy act called 'Laura Laughs'.

By the time he'd gotten back to the hotel the previous evening both of Liam's friends were out for the count. Fast asleep on top of his bedsheets and still fully clothed, Graeme's cheeks blew in and out a shade of red to match his designer shirt. He'd either caught a bit of the sun, or more than likely overworked them with his huffing and puffing over their errant friends' ongoing antics. His bedraggled sandy brown hair perfectly demonstrated his stress as his hands had been run through it a thousand times. There was no gel or wax yet invented that would've been able to cope.

Up and ready to go out since sunrise a trip downstairs for an early breakfast had occupied him for a short time, however, Liam was now pacing back and forth in his room with other things on his mind. When some of last night's nastier flashbacks were shouted down by the thunderous roar of snoring, he knew it was time to get out. It was too early yet for what he wanted to do, but he had itchy feet. Liam wanted to go back to the café where he'd first encountered Laura.

During the flight out here whilst his mate was being a tool to one of the flight attendants, Liam had vowed to use any free time to go and look for his stray friends Mark and Gareth. He suspected they might still take their holiday, only to hide away at the other end of the island to save themselves from being exposed. He had no extravagant plans set in place if he did find them, he just wanted them to know what he knew - they were both pricks. A change in circumstance meant Liam had no time now to waste looking for absentee knobheads, there were far more important things to be getting on with. He wanted to go and see Laura. He needed to see Laura.

Strolling around the main strip on his own was becoming something of a habit for him, but it did at least offer Liam an opportunity to clear his head. It was still early, and he wasn't sure what time Laura's café opened, but ten o'clock am would surely be a more than respectable time to show up unannounced. Neither did he want to come across as being too keen. Nine-forty-five at the very earliest might be okay too.

To see some drunks who'd been too paralytic to make it back to their hotels and were now laid out cold on public benches (one of whom had an uneaten kebab across his chest), Liam thought life perhaps wasn't so bad. Regardless of anything else that might happen on this holiday, he wouldn't be going home to impress his asshole workmates with extravagant and mythical stories of lads on the rampage. The guy sleeping with the kebab had pissed himself. What happens in Tenerife, stays in Tenerife.

Torn between his guilty smile and anguished inhibition, Liam plumped instead for cool detachment.

It was only ten past nine and a group of four lads were already finishing off their breakfasts. As Laura was standing at another table taking an order from a couple, a less than helpful little sign told Liam he could have gotten there an hour earlier. Best not to come across as too keen though, play it cool. Having sat down without giving it much consideration, as his thoughts and his eyes were elsewhere, Liam contemplated jumping up from his chair to go and sit in another. However-

After glancing across to acknowledge the arrival of another customer, and one she vaguely recognised, Laura for the second time asked the couple to repeat their order. As she tried in vain to remember this guy's name she also wondered why, with a choice of four coloured chairs to choose from he'd sat himself down in a pink one. She may not have remembered his name, but perhaps he was more confident than she'd originally given him credit for. Either that or gay.

With a pencil in one hand and a pad in her other, Laura's arms swayed back and forth as she made her way to Liam's table. Between her head bowing down intermittently and Liam's casual looks to one side, neither saw the others smile. When their eyes did eventually meet, Laura caught her feet to stumble forward. Managing to catch a hold of herself before she crashed into Liam's table, with flushed cheeks contradicting her poise Laura dusted herself down. When brushing off her chagrin she noted with interest that Liam had jumped up from his pink chair and was stood ready to catch her. With no catch required he stood stock still with both hands held out in front of him.

'Alright sailor, at ease.' Accusing eyes and an orderly nod of Laura's head suggested Liam could close his open fingers and withdraw his hands to sit down.

'Are you okay?' he asked, whilst doing as he was told.

'Yeah, I'm fine,' Laura began, without making direct eye contact. 'You know what it's like out here. Too much of the wet stuff last night.' When arching her back and tipping her head backward she raised the hand that held her pencil up to her mouth.

'Ah, right. Okay. Cool,' laughed Liam. 'I wish I'd hung around last night. I could have bought you a drink, and maybe spoken to you then.'

Laura's writing hand flopped to her side and as quick as a flash she'd straightened up again. Her actions suggested she'd sobered-up, or at least needed more information.

'I saw you last night. At Yosser's bar. Laura laughs.'

Laughing anxiously as Laura stared down at him, suspicious of his motives or intent, Liam was going to have to fill in some of the gaps. When reminding Laura she'd told him and his two mates she was a comedian, he confessed that he wasn't sure if he'd believed her. She could have been saying it to rile his mate. The one with the tan, Michael Jackson. Liam held back from giving out a high-pitched 'woo-hoo', even though he'd really wanted to. He explained in greater detail how that clown of a mate had got himself pissed drunk and had been a pest, before puking everywhere. His other friend Graeme had to take him back to their hotel. Those events had combined to leave him free to wander the island, and after a while he'd found himself standing outside Yosser's bar.

'Don't you remember me?' asked Liam, when he held out his hand to shake.

After releasing her hand from Liam's, with an inquisitive squint in her eye, Laura scribbled onto her pad. Unless it was nervous energy it could only have been his name she'd written down, as he hadn't given her any breakfast order. Surely, she didn't think he was a stalker? Worst case scenario the cops would at least have a Christian name for a starter clue, if any wrongdoing were to happen.

'I'm flattered Liam, I really am. But I live and work out here so I'm not. Well I'm not looking for any holiday romance.'

'Neither am I,' replied Liam, as he almost choked. Although judging by Laura's change of demeanour he may have offended. 'I didn't mean to,' Liam paused to gather himself, before going on again. 'I'm sorry. You're a very attractive woman and I bet you get hit on all the time. And let's be honest, it'll usually be by asshole men like my friend. Not Graeme, he's a sound bloke. The other one, Michael Jackson. Although I don't mean to say you attract – It's just – well-'

'It's not just the men,' smiled Laura to put Liam out of his misery. She sensed he was being sincere, and in all probability, he probably wasn't a stalker. 'Are you gay?'

Liam's laughter eventually lost the battle with his shaking head. 'Thanks. But no, I'm not gay. Don't worry though, it does seem to be a common misconception nowadays. The problem is, I think. I'm not a bull. Or as I prefer to put it - Not full of bull. I should have been clearer from the outset.' Laura's arms folding across her chest as her hips swung one way and her head the other encouraged Liam to clear up the confusion. 'I'm interested in your comedy, your writing. I've been writing bits and bobs myself, but I don't know anyone back home who does anything like this. Entertainment I mean. Writing, or performing.'

'Bits and bobs! What do you do for a living?' Powered by her shifting eyes, Laura's hips and head switched sides.

Liam hoped there would be several things on the menu that tasted better than her pencil. And Laura's sardonic response hadn't been lost on him either. He'd never been confident enough to tell anyone about his secret passion for writing, not even his friends had any clue. To publicly declare any ambition to be a writer, for a working-class boy like Liam, would be akin to telling all and sundry that he aspired to be a dancer or a nurse. He understood of course that it was all traditional and pretentious bourgeois bullshit, but there it was. Fighting the urge to curl up into a ball in his little pink chair he shouted out the first thing that came to mind. 'I'm a civil servant.'

'So, you work for HMRC. You're a taxman.'

'That's not what I said,' laughed Liam, as he slowly uncoiled himself. It was now a matter of self-defence.

'You said you're a servant. Anyone who's happy to declare themselves a *servant* must be so embarrassed about their job they try to hide it underneath a fraudulent and all-encompassing title. Like those people who work for the tax office. They turn up on corny television game shows and call themselves servants, until they're outed by the jolly host to a round of pantomime boos from the audience.'

Trying not to laugh at Laura's impersonation of a booing crowd, with her hands cupped around her mouth and a knee in the air, Liam knew he should come back with a clever retort. Unfortunately, 'I'm not a taxman,' was all he had. His smile and general body language were a white flag being raised in surrender and Laura thought it would be cruel to torture him anymore. 'Okay, so you're a traffic warden. What can I get for you? Flatfoot.' It was too easy.

His laughter should have bought him time to come back with something witty but didn't. 'I think those people want a word with you.' With no sign of a comeback in sight Liam hoped to use the couple who'd just given their order to Laura as an escape plan, with a little dignity. He could then claim the outcome of this tete-a-tete as a score-draw.

'They'll be alright, they're married.' Laura didn't bother to turn around. Deciding instead to check on the damage she'd inflicted onto her splintered pencil she noticed the eraser on top had gone missing. When she ran her tongue around her gums, she still couldn't find it. 'They'll be so pissed off and annoyed with me they'll probably have sex later. And not for a birthday, or on Christmas. They'd thank me - if they knew what I was doing for them.'

'Wow!'

'I know, it's a gift. Tell me then, what do you write about?'

As soon as he opened his mouth to talk about his writing, Liam knew he'd put his foot in it. He was certain to be mocked again as soon as he finished speaking, so decided to rattle on for a good while longer instead. By indiscriminately mentioning a range of subjects and genres covered in his scribblings he hoped Laura would go easy on him. Whilst still rambling on and sitting underneath the interrogation lights of Laura's eyes, he wondered why she was making this so difficult. He also wondered if his chronic smile would give away the fact that he was enjoying himself. It was most likely some psychological thing he assumed, comparable perhaps to the secret alcoholic or gambler who finally comes clean with an admission of truth.

'Politics!'

'Well, yeah. But, and- '

'And what the fuck, please pardon my French, is kitchen-sink drama?'

'Ah now- '

'That all sounds pretty boring if you ask me. No offence and all, but.' Pressing her hand against her mouth Laura feigned an elongated yawn. She'd almost poked her eye out with her pencil when doing so but carried on with her critique regardless, hoping Liam hadn't noticed. 'I mean, I do have to be honest.'

'That's fine,' started Liam, whilst trying not to laugh too hard at Laura's pencil faux pas. 'I like honesty. If you think your arse looks big in something, then don't ask for my opinion. Because I'll tell it to you straight. That's why I'd like to talk to you, in a roundabout sorta way. Although, I mean. Not about the size of your arse.' Jazz hands of apology were followed by an adjustment in his chair before Liam could go on. 'To perhaps get some honest and impartial feedback on my writing. Not on my genres, or my job. Although again, just for the record. I'm neither a taxman nor a traffic warden.'

Her furrowed brow and curled lip were evidence enough for Liam to say no more for the time being, as he'd at least got Laura to think. Unless, 'fuuuuuuuck,' he thought. Had he just told her she had a fat arse? He'd waffled so much he couldn't recall half of what he'd said, or why. What the fuck was wrong with him? And why would he say something like that? Idiot!

'Most of the stuff I do is observational. And I don't write much of anything down, other than breakfast orders. Are you having a breakfast? And I'll have a think.'

'Coffee please. White, large. To go, please.'

So happy was he to have gotten even a hint of something positive, Liam had no regrets in asking for a takeaway drink. If he'd asked for a breakfast on top of the one he'd already eaten he probably couldn't have finished it. And he wouldn't want to offend, at least no more than he already might have. So jittery was he, imagine what trouble he could find himself in if he hung around any longer. On reflection though he should have ordered an iced drink instead of a coffee. He'd have to go straight back to the hotel to change his top as he was sweating buckets. Liam knew he'd have to open-up and talk to someone about his passion for writing at some point, but never for one second did he imagine it would turn him into a quivering little schoolboy. He'd have to compose himself and be a little cooler when Laura came back out. Much cooler.

'Hey!'

Wearily staring at his feet whilst deep in thought, Liam raised his head to see why Laura had shouted back. As she walked toward the cafe, and on recognising she once again had eye contact with Liam, she dispensed a mischievous grin. Using the index fingers of each hand she then pointed directly toward her white stretched canvas trousers. When a mishmash of shock and embarrassment caused Liam to look up and away from where she was pointing, her bum, he was besieged and overwhelmed to be faced once again with the most scintillating smile and those emerald green eyes. The episode lasted no more than a millisecond, and then she was gone.

To make any sense of his feelings and emotions Liam would need a month to think, a good dictionary and a thesaurus. Either that or his mate Graeme who was good with the words. Where are your mates when you need them? Try as he might, the thing Liam couldn't shake and the only words that came to his mind were, peach, peach, peach. Idiot! This woman was so perceptive, confident, intelligent and rip-roaringly funny, if it hadn't been clear to him before - it was now. Writing aside, Liam was going to have to up his game significantly to get anywhere near her. Probably best not to ask for any advice from Graeme though. Sure he was a champ with the words, but he wasn't much use when it came to girls.

Battle ready with a kitchen utensil in one hand Pauline's other hand was outstretched waiting for an order chitty. Her look of confusion when no chitty was passed on wasn't too dissimilar to Laura's.

'It's two breakfasts. One with brown bread toast and the other without shrooms. And two espresso's – Married couple, fussy buggers. Who'd have guessed? Oh, and a coffee to go. To go – fuck sake!'

Swishing her fish-slice around in her hand Pauline watched on studiously when Laura filled up the kettle before switching it on with attitude. When she then slid it across the stainless-steel worktop and only the mains lead connecting it to the wall stopped it from falling onto the floor, she gave out a shriek. All the while Pauline's free hand followed the mumbling Laura around the kitchen, still waiting for the official order chitty that never came.

'I'll do the breakfasts and you can take out his coffee. To go he said, it's the guy from yesterday.'

'Ooh,' purred Pauline, as she adjusted herself. With her fish-slice still at the ready she hoisted up her jeans before giving her boobs a little perk-up. 'Should I go out and ask him if I can sit on his face? I should, shouldn't I. Oh I don't know. What do you think?'

'No, you will not,' said Laura, with enough bite to cause Pauline to withdraw. 'Sorry. No. It's not the guy who was wearing the New Order t-shirt.' she continued, but in a more conciliatory tone. Looking at her order pad to see again the names she already knew were written there, she went on. 'Graeme's his name, the guy you liked. No, it's one of the others.'

'Oh, okay. Trump?' sighed Pauline through her derisory frown. Breathing easy again she made herself a little less comfortable in her jeans.

'No,' laughed Laura. 'The other one. The interesting one, Liam.' A glance again at the underlined name on her order chitty confirmed what she'd remembered anyway. 'He wants a coffee, to go he said. I'll make it and you can take it out to him.'

After tearing off the top chitty from her pad, Laura folded it in half twice before tucking it into the tiny little pocket that sat above the actual pocket on her trousers. So that's what those things are for!

5

'Bottoms up.'

After necking two of her own shots, Laura had to nudge Pauline to remind her of the rules of this drinking game. Pointing to the latest culprit who, after forgetting how short her skirt had looked in her hotel room, and now tugged on its hem to give herself that all-important extra centimetre of cover for the top of her thighs, Laura urged Pauline to drink up. Sat on high at a little table on a veranda they had a grand view of all the comings and goings on the busy strip below. It was early yet, but there'd already been a steady stream of offenders.

With a sigh Pauline complied to down both of her sickly-sweet beverages too, but she clearly wasn't in the mood to play or to drink anymore. This seemed a little strange as tonight's last-minute night-out had been all her idea.

'It's ten minutes after the last time you looked,' said Laura, when Pauline stared at her watch for the umpteenth time. She hadn't been great company so far, and there was a giant bar of unopened Toblerone in the apartment. Laura wished they'd stayed at home to watch an old movie and eat chocolate.

'What's it all about Laura?'

'Okay. You're obviously drunk already, and a little depressed. That's not a good combo, let's go home.'

Half-standing as she spoke, Laura also made a grab for her jacket. She didn't care about the row of shots waiting to be drunk, she cared about her best mate. After putting on her jacket she gave Pauline's back a tender rub, and in a soothing tone she again suggested they go home.

Reminding her of the unopened Toblerone in their sitting-room, Laura proposed they go home to demolish it in one sitting - whilst watching an old movie.

'Bottoms up,' shouted Pauline out of the blue, to ignore Laura's yearnings. She'd emptied first and then slammed two plastic receptacles back down onto the table. After wiping away the spillage on her bottom lip she pointed to another woman who was tugging furiously at her skirt. 'Come on you,' she said. With her mood now lifted to a certain extent, Pauline seemed ready to stay and play. And to talk. Laura kept her jacket on just in case, but she sat back down to listen when her friend began to open-up.

'I know you don't want to think about the future, and I know why. Please don't fall out with me.' Taking hold of Laura's arm into her hands before resting her head onto her shoulder Pauline looked up to admire the evening sky, but it was too early yet to see the stars. 'The thing is,' she began again. 'I'm bored. We've been out here for a few years now, and I think.' Pauline removed her head from Laura's shoulder to summarise her feelings with magnificent triviality. 'I want some company Laura, I need a bloody man. And not some holiday romance bullshit, I want a proper relationship.'

After sinking another two of her own shots Laura thought her taste-buds might have gone to pot, they'd both tasted rather sour. That giant bar of Toblerone was sounding more appetising with each passing second. Sliding her elbow across the table until her upper arm lay flat on it and planting her head into her hand to look into Pauline's eyes, Laura waited and hoped for the inspiration to find the correct words. With little to no formal education to call on, she would have to use her brains.

'They're here!'

The unexpected burst of enthusiasm from Pauline blew Laura's head from her hand and caused her to slide forward in fright. 'Who's here?' she asked, after gathering herself to look around the strip.

'Bottoms up,' smiled Pauline, before downing another two of her shots, although she hadn't offered any evidence of culprits. 'You're late,' she shouted excitedly over Laura's shoulder.

'Late! Who's late?' Laura had no idea who or what she was looking for and couldn't see anyone they knew.

'Late! Late for what?' asked Graeme, when hearing Pauline's excitement. Unsure of what was going on, he wasn't much for putting in a protest either. He nudged an elbow into Liam's side to elicit a reply, and neither he nor Liam noticed the flopping hands and fabricated sighs of exasperation from their drunk and volatile friend.

'I might have told him,' began Pauline, through a blend of apology and enthusiasm. 'When I took him out his coffee, that we might be here tonight.'

Unimpressed to have been kept out of the loop, Laura picked up another two shots to down them in quick succession. 'Bottoms,' she groaned.

'Bottoms up.' Oblivious to Laura's current mood, or wordplay, Pauline played along eagerly to sink another two shots nimbly. She was too busy grinning to look for any offending girls.

'You're late,' bellowed Pauline again, with Graeme and Liam stood below her and now within earshot. Still though, they could only just about hear her over the three different techno tunes from three different bars blending into one mundane metronome.

'Late for what?' Graeme whispered to his left one more time, but with Liam suddenly looking a little distant he didn't want to push too hard. Unfortunately, up to this point this had been the holiday from hell they'd both expected.

'Laura's mate, Pauline. She told me they might be coming here for a drink tonight.' Liam's words sneaked out from the side of his mouth. It was one of the worst ventriloquist performances you've never seen. Graeme supposed that was why Liam hadn't turned to look at him when doing it, his eyes never left Laura's.

'Did I say that I might have mentioned something to Liam, when I took out his coffee?' asked Pauline again, when turning to Laura. For a second time she got no reply, because she hadn't told Laura anything. Besides, Laura and Liam already seemed to be playing off against one-another in some weird ad-hoc staring competition. It appeared to be a good-natured encounter though, Pauline had no great headache in working out that both competitors were trying hard to contain their merriment.

'I didn't even - No-one told me anything.' Graeme tried to plead his innocence whilst double-taking his look between Laura and Liam for help. He got no support from Liam, and no comfort either. Wondering what was going on with his mate, and ignorant to the cause of the uncomfortable silence between him and Laura, Graeme pondered getting the two of them out of there. On the verge of hinting that they had to be somewhere else for something else, his quivering knees stopped him from doing-so. That, and-

'I liked your t-shirt the other day. Liam told me they're your favourite band. New Order.'

If any were needed, Pauline's compliment was irrefutable evidence that there'd been more to this evening than a random, 'oh how do you do' bumping into one another event. Another discreet glance toward Liam reassured Graeme there was nothing untoward going on with him and Laura after-all. Besides, Liam could handle himself. To hell with going anywhere else, this was the hottest place in town.

'Your mate, what's his face?' Laura conceded defeat in her game with Liam but did so with reason and a purpose. 'He's an arsehole,' she continued, when pointing over Liam's shoulder.

The grin of victory was wiped from Liam's face when he turned around to see what Laura was pointing at. He needn't have bothered turning as he'd a fair idea what would be facing him when he did. Graeme didn't bother to turn, 'It's my night off,' he said, when copying his friends vaudeville act. It was Liam's turn to fetch and look after the dummy tonight, and Graeme's turn now to play whatever game Liam had been playing with Laura. And Pauline was a more than willing adversary.

'They might well be looking for it. Why else would they run away from the gossiping tongues back home to come here for two weeks, other than to explore their sexuality guilt free? However, that doesn't mean they're asking for it, there's a difference. And certainly NOT from him.' Laura's stinging words were delivered with the punch of a professional boxer giving their pre-bout press conference. Half-standing as she'd shouted them, they were intended to go over Graeme's head and direct to the departing Liam. She succeeded in at least one of her aims.

'It's my night off,' Graeme repeated, when he'd heard someone say something about somebody else. Too wrapped up in his own affairs to know who'd said what about whom, and still unsure of the rules of the game he was playing with Pauline, Graeme at least needed to confirm to all and sundry his intentions regarding any erratic mates. Pauline's yellow trousers as one of her crossed legs flashed back and forth underneath her table should have grabbed the attention. Her lustrous blue eyes confined them to a minor supporting role, whilst her dazzling smile lit up the early-evening sky.

'Anywhere in the world, including here. At any time, that is sexual assault.'

Even with his back turned to her, Liam knew Laura wasn't smiling anymore, and no longer was she in the mood for playing silly games. Her words and tone of voice were the perfect commentary for what he was now witnessing, a most imperfect scenario. Two young ladies who were no doubt just looking for a decent night out were having to constantly brush his friends hands away from their arses and off their waists. The strip was a bustling arena and yet only he and Laura seemed to notice what was going on. It could, and probably would be argued by some that it was a sensory overload from all the loud sounds, the flashing lights and shimmering dresses that distracted people from seeing this abuse. On the other-hand it could also be argued that this offence was such common practise now, it was part of the norm.

On their way here tonight any glimpse of a woman's bare flesh had brought about an uncouth and unwelcome approach from Liam and Graeme's wayward friend. Graeme's happy whistling had at times been replaced by a grungy hum, and It was only now that Liam recognised the tune he'd been humming. It was 'The Road to Hell'.

Graeme was happier yet when Pauline shouted out, 'bottoms up,' before downing two little shots. If she was playing a game, she wasn't overly obsessed with winning. Her hair though dark grabbed a hold of the light from somewhere and it shone, and she may have had her nose pierced at some point, but Graeme was most taken by what looked like a little birthmark above her left eyebrow. She herself would probably be self-conscious when talking about this, but Graeme thought it was shaped like a little heart.

After standing up and blindly reaching out to the back of her seat for the jacket she'd already put on, Laura urged Pauline to join her. From experience she knew there were six steps to walk down to street level, which was just as well as at all times she kept at least one eye on how Liam was dealing with his friend. He was doing okay. It probably hadn't been the liberation they'd come to Tenerife for, but both ladies had at least been set free. The tables had been turned and Liam was now manhandling his friend. Unsurprisingly, the prick wasn't so keen on it himself.

'Can I buy you a drink?' Unable to suppress his disappointment to watch Pauline follow Laura down the steps and past him, the tone of Graeme's voice didn't make for the most appealing of invitations. He had to say something though, and in his current state that was all he had.

'Next time,' smiled Pauline, when she turned around to walk toward Graeme. 'If I am going to be tempted into making questionable choices, I'd much rather do it when I'm sober.' When wrapping her hands tight onto and around the top of Graeme's corresponding arms Pauline continued with a sparkle. 'What's your favourite New Order song?'

'The perfect kiss,' Graeme almost whispered, without meaning to.

When Pauline threw her head back to look up into the cloudless lavender sky and her hands tightened their grip on his arms, Graeme's instinct was to reach out and stop her from falling back. Such was her hold on him he couldn't move a muscle, even if he'd needed to. It was still early but when Pauline looked up, she thought she could see the stars aligning.

'Next time,' Pauline began again when lowering her glare. And with a gentle tap of her index finger against Graeme's nose to accentuate each word, she spoke softly. 'Don't. Be. Late.'

It could have been seconds, minutes or even hours for all he knew, but as he again tried to comprehend what was happening Graeme scrambled for words. He loved anything to do with wordplay and games associated with such, and historically he'd work experience in sales teams and been trained on using the five W's. The who, what, why, where and when. But right now when he needed them most, every one of those W's was engaged in a brutal civil war within his befuddled brain.

'When?' eventually won the battle, and Graeme shouted over the crowd to the departing Pauline. As she was being led away arm in arm with Laura and just about to exit stage left, Graeme shouted louder still. 'You said next time. When?'

Freeing up her arms without breaking stride, Pauline danced around to face Graeme again. 'Mine is Temptation,' she shouted back. 'In case you were wondering.' she concluded with a playful curtsey, before turning again to skip off into the setting sun with Laura.

6

After yet another debacle of a night-out, and one that had initially shown some promise, it had been decided by majority vote that today would be a day without alcohol. This evening would be spent relaxing by the hotel pool. Before any of that they'd have a spot of lunch in a café. By unanimous vote this time (only two votes were counted), it was deemed too embarrassing to show up at Laura and Pauline's LP's café. Instead, they would go somewhere to watch old episodes of Only Fools and Horses on a loop. That would cheer everyone up.

An older gentleman at a nearby table had Liam wondering why people on holiday felt the need to buy and read their favourite tabloids from back home. Not only were they reading yesterday's newspapers telling them yesterday's lies, they were paying five times the face price for the privilege. How embarrassingly British. Liam offered a friendly nod to the old gent when he lowered his newspaper from his face, he may have sensed he was being watched. After carefully adjusting his glasses back onto the sunburnt nose on his long pink face, the old fella resumed his reading. He sensed no immediate threat from the potential yobs sat opposite him, but he'd be watching.

Graeme had been reticent for most of the morning. It was most likely due to his tempestuous, albeit brief falling out with Liam the night before. In fairness to Liam, after Pauline had left the scene and when he'd asked Graeme to 'shut the fuck up', it had been preceded with a 'please'. They'd had far worse debates over the years for sure, but never one so far from home. This one felt different. Following his reprimand the previous evening, Graeme had then decided to position himself a good five or six feet behind his two mates. Thanks to this neither of his mates could hear his constant mutterings. Additionally though, if he had been tempted to swing a punch or throw out a kick it wouldn't have connected with anyone. Safety first.

After returning to their hotel the previous evening Liam did eventually get to brush his teeth and have a wash. He was the only one of the three to do so. Before he could even do that, he'd had to bring down the toilet seat after flushing away his mates waste, and there was a puddle of piss on the tiled floor that needed mopping up. He didn't want to leave it for the cleaner, or worse still forget about it and walk through it in his bare feet during the night. His final babysitting task of the evening had been to remove the trainers from the feet of his friend who was out cold already. He was going to remove his socks too, until with one finger and a thumb he'd felt dampness between the toes and decided against it. It was at that point he'd decided not to throw a blanket over the twat.

Graeme had already barged his drunken mate out of the way to be the first one in the bathroom. He'd then ripped off his clothes to hurl them onto the floor by his bed and with his head tucked underneath a pillow he'd hidden himself away in the foetal position. As he'd looked at his best mate before switching off the bedroom light Liam had smiled. He'd no idea when he'd heard him talking in the toilet, if Graeme had been castigating their mate remotely or chastising himself. He'd heard him say out loud repeatedly, 'It was my fucking night off.'

Loose lips sink ships, and they can also rejuvenate pent-up frustrations. As such Liam was delighted with the deafening silence that allowed him the time and space to clear his head. It's far easier to have a spring-clean of the mind in quiet surroundings. Why are so many people so afraid of being alone? Even for a short period of time, relatively speaking.

There was no debating that up until now this was, and most likely would be until it's conclusion, one of the shittiest times of Liam's life so far. And yet to contradict this, as he took another sip of his long macchiato, Liam had never been so sure he was in the right place at the right time, right now. He was precisely where he was supposed to be. Where he needed to be.

7

It was one of those rare *three bears* kind of days. Neither too hot nor too cold, it was just right. As a result it had been a quiet day with only a few customers and nothing of much note to talk about.

Laura's tummy had been giving her jip all morning. Bent down and across the café counter she would occasionally thrust herself forward and onto its edge. She hoped the two customers she did have in wouldn't notice her weird gyrations or hear the rumblings in her gut that at times threatened to explode. Thankfully, they seemed to be so loved-up they probably wouldn't have noticed had she stood up on the counter and raised a leg to fart and burp at the same time. Pauline certainly wouldn't have noticed, and she wasn't making herself available to talk either. All morning she'd been busying herself with those little jobs that are sometimes forgotten about during the busier times. With a bottle of all-purpose surface cleaner in one hand and a microfibre cloth in her other, she sprayed and wiped as she shuffled her feet across the now shiny tiled floor. She hummed along with the tunes on her i-pod as she went. Today's silent disco was a continuation of the one she'd enjoyed the previous evening.

When returning home from their short-lived night out, Laura had sat herself in front of the television while Pauline played and danced along to some of her favourite vinyl records. For a short while it had been a strange sight to behold as the volumes of the television and the record player fought for supremacy. After Laura had declared herself unwell to take herself off to bed, Pauline turned up the volume on her record player from three to five. She was left alone to dance herself into the wee small hours.

Still bent over the counter with her muted groans, Laura saw Bill and Christina approaching the courtyard of the café. She couldn't recall if she'd ever watched them as closely, although she'd probably remember because they were regular as clockwork. Resplendent in his freshly pressed white shirt Bill was all gentleman. His left arm was held out proud in front for it to be entwined with his good ladies right arm, whilst the pink parasol she held in her left hand multi-tasked as a walking aid. Gliding in her flared and flowing summer dress, Christina's sense of fashion and style belied her years. She looked glamorous, but truly beautiful too. They were a curious couple Bill and Christina, quite a contradiction. During daylight hours they were all class, but as the sun began to set it signalled a change in them. A force of habit no doubt, due in part to those swinging-sixties. What a time that must have been to be alive.

Given the time to choose where she wanted to sit, Bill then used his handkerchief to dust down Christina's chair of choice. Accepting her hand into his own and with his free hand supporting her back he helped to ease her down onto her temporary throne. With Christina no longer by his side to give him balance, Bill's walk was similar in style to a performing horse doing dressage. In keeping his back as straight as possible his knees would rise straight up before then kicking out his legs to take each step. It was a side-effect of some historic medical affair he and Laura had discussed at great length.

To shout out, 'lunch for B and C' today, would have been an exercise in futility. A quick glance was enough to confirm that Pauline was still immersed in dance. Presently, she was engaged in an open-fingered raise your hands up 'woop woop' affair. Knowing what a stickler Pauline could sometimes be, Laura wrote out a chitty anyway. On presenting that chitty directly to Bill (before he'd had a chance to ask for, 'just the usual sweetheart'), it was handed over in the style of a magician giving their big *ta-da* finale. Bill winked knowingly when accepting the slip of paper, and when Laura's pointing finger revealed Pauline shuffling by the open doorway to the kitchen. When crouching down, Bill pressed a finger against his smiling lips.

A loud shriek of 'holy shit' was quickly followed by 'Christ is that the time?' Those squeals did concern briefly the coffee drinking couple, but they were re-assured when Laura hadn't budged an inch from her squat position on the counter. Unbeknown to them, she was afraid to.

Bill wouldn't have known Pauline was wearing earphones because he didn't need any accompaniment or excuse to have a dance. And Laura needn't have worried about Bill's heart giving out through shock either. In no time at all he and Pauline had cut loose from the kitchen. With her earphones dangling over her shoulders and taking a lead from Bill, Pauline went hand to hand with him before being spun around. Bill danced better than he walked, it came naturally to him. The momentum of one final spin took Pauline back toward her kitchen and with reddening cheeks she took a bow, before vanishing again.

Presenting his arm out straight before slowly turning his wrist, Bill offered his hand to Laura. There was plenty of life left in the old dog yet. With a pronounced groan and no little care, Laura hauled herself up from her crouched position to passably caress her tummy.

'Is it the crimson wave sweetheart?' asked Bill, as he slowly withdrew his arm. 'What?' he professed, 'Christina buys the Cosmopolitan, and I read it.' A gentle shake of her head and a smile for the old bugger, because his heart was in the right place, was all Laura could manage.

'Is it your legs again doll?' He was a persistent old so-and-so, but Laura again replied with a shake of her head. She wasn't embarrassed to talk about 'lady issues' with anyone, let alone Bill, he'd seen her stand-up act on numerous occasions. And nor was she too proud to discuss any of her other medical issues. However, her problem today was something she'd rather keep to herself. When making his way into the bathroom Bill held his hands up in surrender. 'If you do want to talk, you know where to find me sweetie.' Poking his head back out from the bathroom with a laugh, with strangers being present he thought it best to clarify, 'not in here though, eh!'

Until Bill had brought it to her attention again Laura had forgotten about the coffee drinking couple. What must they think about everything they'd just witnessed? Holding hands across their table they were most likely fearful for their lives in this madhouse of a café. Assuming they could get themselves out of there alive they more than likely wouldn't be coming back. As the couple stood up from their table, they continued to protect one-another. Laura hadn't seen smiles like theirs in a while. They had to be phoney ones fabricated to confuse the mad shop lady allowing them to make good their escape.

'That was beautiful,' said the man. 'Lush,' added his partner. 'It's so nice to see dancing like that again,' the man continued. 'Old school,' smiled his partner. 'And in public too.'

So comforted was Laura by these lovely comments, and embarrassed for her own pre-judgements, she flopped her arms onto the counter to drop her bellowing tummy down there too. The noises emanating from within were mortifying. 'You should have got up and joined in,' she said, to distract from the turbulence in her tummy.

'No,' the lady shook her head.

'We can't dance,' her partner smiled.

'Everyone can dance,' said Laura. 'You've just forgotten how.'

After they'd handed over two paper notes with an instruction to keep the change, Laura wasn't sure whether the couple had a great time or just knew her tummy was about to blow. Watching the couple leave, Laura caught sight again of Christina who was waiting patiently for her man to return. She was lost without her beloved Bill by her side.

'I'll take these out,' said Pauline, as she danced out from the kitchen with a spin. With a plate of hot food in each hand it was a site to behold. 'I can't stop myself from moving today,' she dazzled.

'Okay,' said Laura with a whimper. 'Less of the quickstep though, Bill's still in the bathroom.' On grabbing hold of her tummy again she then had a change of mind. 'Having said that, don't take too long. I'm desperate for a shit. I knew I shouldn't have eaten all of that Toblerone by myself.'

8

Pauline's idea to leave home early meant they'd taken a more indirect route than was normally the case, through the main strip. Laura had initially agreed as it should have given her some additional time to focus on her material for this evening's performance.

'People who live in Blackpool. Well, they still go out for drinks in Blackpool. Don't they?'

Between Pauline's mundane questions, her own 'uhu-uhu-ing' and even more non-committal answers of 'whatever', Laura wasn't getting the rehearsal time she'd hoped for. Thankfully, Pauline wasn't too interested in any of the skewed answers she'd been getting in reply. She was too busy rubbernecking the strip.

'We should definitely go out a little more than we do though, we're still young. I propose from here on we go out once a week. At least, starting tomorrow.'

'U-hu.'

Surrounded by locals they knew and those who thought they knew her from seeing her act that one time, Laura and Pauline didn't get much peace. There were also the guys who imagined they looked like Brad Pitt, dressed like David Beckham, sang like Marvin Gaye and danced like Prince. Ah, the magical properties of alcohol. Pauline's mind was undeniably elsewhere and she hadn't noticed anything untoward, but Laura had chosen to wear a shorter skirt than usual this evening. As a result she was taking the full brunt of it. I mean, a short skirt! What the fuck had she expected to happen? Right?

Running to the bar when they got to Yosser's, to lean across the counter and shout 'hiya', Pauline was buoyant when seeing Yoz. She'd alerted others to her arrival too. Returning his own hushed hello before placing an index finger against his gurning lips, Yoz's other hand pointed timidly toward the little stage. On turning around to face the music, literally, Pauline offered a hand of apology to Dusty who was halfway through her rousing version of 'I'm every woman'. Carrying on like a battle-hardened professional, Dusty's contempt was transferred instead to the crowd of unappreciative lowbrow's sat in front of her. Following Dusty's lead drew Pauline's eyes to Bill, he was stood by his table and waving wildly over Christina's head. Unable to resist his infectious joy, Pauline sent back her own exuberant hello that she'd wrapped up in a sexy kiss to blow his way. Christina's initial concern turned to laughter after she'd managed to stop Bill from falling over when he'd tried and failed to catch Pauline's kiss in mid-air.

When Laura caught up with Pauline, she wondered what she'd been doing to offer one hand of apology to the merry widows, whilst her other was held out submissively towards the stage. As Dusty sang through a grimace, her lyrics of 'mixing a special brew' and 'putting a fire inside of you' were all aimed at Pauline. With intent.

Busily running bits of her act through her head still, Laura didn't look to anyone specifically when asking without feeling if things were 'alright'.

'Good, the two of you together. I need some advice.' Yoz beckoned Laura and Pauline to come in a little closer to avoid upsetting Dusty any further. 'I'm thinking about changing the clientele in here. I'm going to go after the young team, those with a bit of cash to spend,' he whispered with a sly grin before settling himself back into his wheelchair. 'Either that or the gays.'

'Change the clientele?' A shocked Pauline wanted confirmation, but she'd looked to Laura when speaking.

Laura wondered why Pauline was looking to her for an answer, before she herself asked for clarification, 'the young team?'

'Yeah,' stated Yoz, with an air of authority. He also had the look of a scoundrel about him, to pre-warn that he was about to go into more detail. 'The spit-roasting, gang-banging, head-bobbing, blow-jobbing and shag happy young team.'

'Yoz!' cried Pauline.

'What is wrong with you?' Laura challenged.

'The two of you are stuck in your ways. You've no fucking imagination.'

'Now that you come to mention it. I was thinking along the same lines, about the two of us,' started Pauline. She was stopped in her tracks by an anxious look from Laura, and a devilish one from Yoz.

'I'm not – I don't mean – Not the head bobbing – oh fuck-off Yoz. Both of you.' As her eyes began to scan the bar, in part to mask her bashfulness, Pauline began again. 'I'm talking about the younger crowd. Have you had any in lately? Three guys maybe?' As she hadn't turned around to ask the question, Pauline didn't see the suggestive and questioning countenance behind the bar.

'Some guy called Liam,' smiled Laura, as she mock whispered over the bar. The hand she'd held against her cheek when doing so was batted away when Pauline did turn around to see it.

'Well now,' with little discretion, Pauline began again. Leaning across the bar counter she began to mock whisper herself. 'That Yoz, is what they call a Freudian slip. For what it's worth, the guy I was referring to is called Graeme.'

'Who are these philandering young ladies-men?' enquired a cross-eyed Yoz. 'And more importantly, do they have any money - And a taste for alcohol?'

'We'll talk about this later.' Laura put on her game face as Dusty began to belt out her impassioned encore. 'Both of you,' she continued, whilst wagging an accusing finger. 'Dim the lights a little more Yoz, nice and slow. And let Dusty know to play along.'

Heading off with stealth, Laura shook her head. She could hear Pauline being asked if a Freudian slip was an exotic form of sexy lingerie.

'And I need to borrow this one,' demanded Laura. Grabbing hold of a shirt-sleeve of the young bartender who'd been slouched across the bar enjoying the exchanges between Yoz and the girls, Laura hauled him towards the ladies toilets. Manuel's amusement was displaced by confusion.

'Ladies and gentlemen, you know the fucking score. No photographs and no filming - for security reasons.' Adjusting her eyes to a room that was a little darker than usual, Dusty could see no sign of Laura. What she did see, and wondered why, was Pauline waving her hands up and down whilst making demented faces. Wheeling himself out from behind the bar, Yoz calmly rolled his hands around and around. This coupled with a nodding head and a genial smile allowed Dusty to carry on with her introduction. Albeit a little addled, and still looking for Laura, that's what she did.

'Please, everyone. Put your hands together and welcome your favourite and my favourite dirty girl – ladies and gentlemen, It's Laura laughs.'

Dropping her hand with the microphone held tight in it down to her side, Dusty, like everyone else looked around the room. She'd seen Laura not five minutes since, but wherever she looked now, there was no sign of her.

Inside the ladies toilets Laura ruffled the still shaking Manuel's hair by running her hands back and forth through it. 'Oh look at you. You're a pretty little boy,' she laughed, before unbuttoning his shirt. When pulling open the toilet door with force, and a grin, she shouted out, 'now piss off.' As well as tossing Manuel aside her loud shout and the bang of the toilet door hitting against the back wall drew everyone's attention. The bright lights that emanated from the toilet to shine a light on the fleeing and dishevelled Manuel was a bonus.

'Fucking hell.' With the microphone at her knees, no-one heard Dusty swear.

As Manuel tried to button up his shirt whilst running for cover behind the bar, he couldn't help but glance behind to make sure Laura wasn't following him. He was aided on his way by a clip around the ear from Yoz. Slap aside, he would feel safer behind the bar and well clear of a seemingly rampant Laura. After theatrically fanning her face for a few seconds Laura stepped out from the toilet to let out a loud yelp of 'WOO', before then pretending to catch her breath. Resonantly adjusting her skirt as she began walking toward Dusty, her ungainly and ponderous walk revealed her to be partially hamstrung. She had a pair of skimpy white knickers wrapped around her ankles.

'Fucking hell.' Again, no-one heard Dusty swear. The microphone she held at her knees was almost dropped in shock, and behind her the squeals of laughter were ear-splitting. Holding out her free hand to help Laura up the little step and onto the stage, Dusty could feel Laura trying to prise the microphone out from her hand.

All the while, both were careful to keep those scanty little panties exactly where they were.

'Cheers doll.' Laura had to shout, before finally managing to wrestle the microphone from Dusty's clenched fingers.

'What?' After instruction from the audience, those who between fits of hilarity were still able to point, Laura looked down at her ankles. When raising her head again she feigned shock and embarrassment, before looking out and into the crowd to take a moment to herself. Whilst she held a microphone in one hand, there was no doubt she had this audience in the palm of her other.

'Oh, fuck-off. Haven't any of you seen a pair of knickers before?' After relenting with an unplanned laugh herself, Laura bent down to remove the offending undies from her ankles. Placing the microphone between her knees for a second allowed her to stretch out the knicker elastic in her hands. Catapult style, she slung them onto Bill and Christina's table. 'They're edible panties Bill,' she laughed. 'Tuck in.'

So debilitated was she with laughter when Bill lifted the panties to put them in his mouth, Laura was lost for words. Although she couldn't tell him the panties weren't edible, he seemed to work it out for himself when he spat them out onto his table. Alongside his dentures.

In a rare moment of hush generated through a collective breathlessness, Christina was heard to shout, 'you can think again, if you think that tongue is coming anywhere near me tonight.'

'As if.' With two words Laura drew the attention away from a repentant Bill and back onto herself. 'Poor wee Manuel,' she continued. 'I did try, but I couldn't get him to do anything with me in those toilets. I'm not kidding. I'm so fucking desperate and it's been that long since I had a shag, I think my vadge has grown teeth. Honestly, the angry little bastard is biting away at the top of my thighs as we speak.' Soaking up the laughter, Laura thrust a hand inside her skirt to rub at the top of her thighs. The grinding of her teeth was a last-second ad-lib. After then turning her back to her crowd and bending forward, she lifted her little skirt all the way up her back to reveal the oversized granny pants she was wearing. Written large on the backside of these pants, in felt pen, was the name 'BRIDGET'.

'I've no idea why I can't get a shag,' Laura shouted into the microphone. She was still bent over, ogling the audience from between her open legs.

'Does she get extra money for props?' moaned Dusty. She was trying hard not to laugh as she'd said it. 'That's favouritism,' she continued, whilst mopping up some of her spilt drink.

'She has no shame, and I don't know how she does it. But she's hilarious.' Pauline said to Yoz, whilst laughing and shaking her head in unison.

'Yeah, never mind any of that,' was his reply. 'Who's this Liam fella?'

9

Another day, another nightmare in the sun.

With their mate pissed drunk and shouting to anyone who'd care to listen (there weren't many), that he'd arranged a meet-up with Swedish twins for a threesome, Liam and Graeme had done well to hold their peace. They'd found it much harder to hold their tongues. After separating themselves to have a better chance of finding their now wandering friend, Liam and Graeme individually rued the day they'd landed on this island. On the plus-side, every step they took now and every minute that passed brought them a little closer to going home.

Perched on a wall to rest his feet for a while, Liam watched holidaymakers pack away their belongings after another fun filled day on the beach. Looking out onto the deep blue sea and into the horizon he imagined the twilights and sunsets he wouldn't witness. It wouldn't be near the top of most men's lists of things to do and see on holiday, but Liam didn't care much for what other's thought.

A shout from behind of, 'hello stranger' was as unexpected as it was welcome. It was quickly followed by a cheery, 'long time no see'.

On turning to confirm who was shouting, Liam saw Pauline grinning from ear to ear. Standing barefoot and carefree she swung two bags of popcorn in one hand and a carry case of six bottles of lager in the other. They both had their hands full, but for very different reasons.

After listening to Liam explain why they'd felt the need to keep their distance, and then laughing off any thoughts of him being a stalker, Pauline assured him they'd be welcome at the café anytime. Him and Graeme, she'd said without thinking. Changing the subject to a certain extent, Pauline went on, 'I think your other mate. I think there might be some underlying issues there.' Pauline tried to reason why Liam was sitting alone on a wall on his holiday. She then asked, as he and Graeme weren't looking for their mate together, where was Graeme? Had they been out chasing the girls the night before, and. Well, you know.

'I think you might be right.'

'What? Graeme's with a girl?'

When he'd finished sniggering, Liam apologised. He assured Pauline that they'd only split up to look for their mate, and that Graeme wasn't with a girl. Observing how demure Pauline had suddenly become he swiftly changed the subject, 'are you having a party?'

'It's movie night, kind of a tradition. If you're not meeting up with your pals?' As Pauline announced her plans for the evening she turned to look to the side, she'd changed again from a state of minor excitement back to a bashful awkwardness. 'You know. If you're not going out with your mate, chasing the birds. Why don't you-'

'The birds!' scoffed Liam, which did at least bring eye contact with Pauline again. 'No, I'm not - We're not chasing the birds. That's not why we came out here. Anyway, wouldn't your friend be pissed off? You know, if you took me back to your apartment on a traditional night?'

'Your friend!' Pauline chuckled. 'Oh. Look at you, pretending you're all shy and can't remember her name. Here,' she said as she thrust the carry case of lager in front of her. 'I'm no Rachel Riley, but I know that six can be divided into three as easily as it can into two. Come on.'

10

'Are you decent?' Pauline's facial expressions, all of them, after shouting along the hall was Liam's first clue that bringing a companion home for movie night wasn't part of the tradition. 'I've got company.'

'Did you bump into your fancy man?' came a shouted reply from behind the closed sitting-room door. It was subsidised with a ballsy laugh that had it been a man would have been accompanied with a scratch to the bollocks. It wasn't a man, it was Laura.

Shooed on up the hall with an erring smile after having three bottles of lager thrust into his sweaty palms, an apprehensive Liam was assured that everything would be fine. 'On you go, it's cool,' said Pauline. She wafted her hands forward before disappearing into the kitchen with the popcorn and remaining bottles of lager. Pausing for a moment to curse that he wasn't more proficient in reading the signals women seem so fond of sending, Liam took in a breath before opening the sitting-room door. He hoped he wasn't going to embarrass himself by dropping a bottle, especially not his own.

'Oh!' retreating from the television, Laura glanced up briefly before slumping down onto a two-seat sofa. 'It's you!' she continued, without bothering to look up again.

Again with the signals. Granted this one had been a little easier to read, albeit in the negative, but Liam wished he had a translator to be sure. Statuesque in the open doorway he was in-part transfixed by Laura's casual appearance, but also because she clearly didn't have a care as to what anybody might think of it. She was wearing what might commonly be referred to as her comfy's. In a baggy old t-shirt, black legging type trousers and wearing no make-up, she continued her ongoing struggle with the remote control.

With Laura unconcerned by his presence Liam received no formal invitation where to sit. Looking around the room there where two choices open to him. There was the vacant space on the sofa next to Laura and in front of the television, or a shabby old thing placed parallel with the TV and facing the two-seater. It was a cosy little place, and not untypical of a woman's sitting-room. Behind the sofa was a handy sized free space for, well whatever really. Hanging on the wall above a little table, where an old record player sat were some arty pictures of female popstars from bygone days, some of whom Liam recognised. There was a pleasant aroma that whilst only teasing the nostrils contradicted the spots of curry sauce on Laura's otherwise off-white t-shirt. Perhaps they'd had an Indian the day before and she hadn't been too fussed about changing.

'Excuse me – coming through.'

Dilemma over. Whilst balancing a bowl of popcorn in one hand Pauline used her other to dim the lights before brushing past Liam. Abruptly awakened from his thoughts he was ordered by Pauline, as she took her place next to Laura, to sit in the chair positioned next to the TV. 'Feel free to move it,' she said. 'If you want to see the telly.'

'You bitch.' A screaming insult from Laura just as Liam was about to sit down, caused him to turn around. 'You've mixed the salty and the sweet together again. Bitch.'

'It's a tradition. You witch.' With the bowl of popcorn resting on her lap, Pauline's raised hand poured scorn on Laura's erroneous insult. And when seeing Liam looking at her, knowing she had an audience, she smiled when sticking out her tongue for good measure.

Liam didn't bother to move his seat and with regards to the movie didn't think he'd missed that much. Although he did recognise some of the songs from the soundtrack (most of which were in Graeme's extensive record collection), the best part of the evening (other than the sight of Laura's squirming face anytime a salty popcorn kernel made its way into her mouth) could only have been witnessed from his position opposite the sofa anyway. There had been a moment when Pauline and Laura grabbed hold of one-another, and when gazing into each other's eyes they both shouted in perfect harmony with a character from the movie, 'love's a bitch Duck. Love's a bitch.'

'Liam hasn't come here for the birds.'

The movie credits had been allowed to play out in their entirety, allowing the theme tune to be played out in full too. It had been accompanied by a zealous though slightly out of tune duet. With their fervid crooning at an end Pauline couldn't contain herself any longer. With a continuation of good cheer she'd shouted her newsflash on Liam's holiday plans. Or lack of them, to be precise.

'Hasn't he,' said Laura, as she grabbed at the remote control to switch off the television. 'He says he's not gay though.'

Waiting for Pauline to take her seat again, Liam held his tongue to prepare for what could be an imminent onslaught. Blinking furiously as Pauline hadn't shown any restraint with her dextrous spin of the dimmer switch, his interrogation was about to begin. He'd forgotten how bright those old style light-bulbs could be.

With four searching eyes bearing down on him, all of them eagerly waiting for an explanation, Liam had no option but to relent. He began by explaining how this holiday had been organised as a duel birthday celebration (two of his mates were going to be twenty-seven during the trip). He told how one of those birthday boys had cancelled at the last minute, but he was a tool anyway, so it didn't matter. The other birthday boy was also a tool, but they'd already met him and knew that. He confided that for him this may also be a rite of passage holiday, as in their friendships had perhaps run their course. 'I think it might just be time to move on.' he said. Finishing his statement with a nervous laugh, Liam wasn't sure why he was being so candid with two women he'd only just met.

'But whilst you're out here!' Laura's statement that doubled as a loaded question was backed up by Pauline. 'Surely!'

With his protestations falling on deaf ears Liam placed his freshly emptied bottle of lager onto the floor. Sitting back to cross his legs, he hoped he'd put an end to the matter.

'Are you sure you're not gay?'

When mirroring Liam to sit back and scrunch herself comfortable, rather than finding a penny down the back of the sofa, Laura found the same question to ask again.

'It's okay if you are.' As she delved into Liam's soul Pauline meant what she'd said. 'We don't mind. We know a gay couple who run one of the bars out here, don't we?' Laura didn't see Pauline looking to her for the affirmation of them being liberal minded and accepting of gay culture. Her eyes instead watched Liam's every blink and every flinch to look for telling clues. 'They're married. Our gay friends I mean.' Pauline summed up with a 'happily ever after' ending.

'So – are you gay?' Unable to see or sense any conclusive signs, Laura came right out and asked her question again. This did at least prevent Pauline from rushing across to give him a grand 'coming out' hug. She'd certainly looked poised to do so.

'I'm not a taxman or a traffic-warden. And I'm not gay. I'm afraid that makes you zero from three.' Rather than shrivelling under the pressure, Liam sat back in cruise control. As he faced off directly with Laura, he could just about see Pauline twitching her look from left to right and back again.

'So, you're single then?' asked Pauline, when she felt compelled to fill an otherwise empty space. Laura's narrowed eyes and Liam's smiling lips were preventing them from saying anything more. 'Single, and straight?' she concluded to answer her own question, whilst her eyes continued their search for a focal point.

'Tell us your last break-up story.' After being reprimanded for her poor judgement on his employment and sexuality, Laura went back on the front foot. It hadn't helped Liam's cause that his smile was becoming a little irritating. 'Your last girlfriend. Why did you break-up?'

Grasping at the bowl of popcorn on her lap, Pauline turned to face Liam again. If it were a game of tennis, the score would be deuce.

When Liam's eyes opened wide, his vexing smile disappeared with a croak. After edging forward in his chair again, a quick glance to the floor confirmed he'd already finished his two bottles of lager. Not wanting to seem ungrateful, and fairly certain the six empty bottles around him were the only supplies in the house, he casually stayed put. He would wait and hope, for a different topic of conversation.

'You'll have to excuse my friend. She's not shy in coming forward I'm afraid.'

Liam's nod of appreciation for Pauline's courteous deferral brought daggers from Laura. Unfortunately for Liam she then went on, 'However, seeing how you nearly choked when asked the question, I'm afraid you're not leaving here until you tell us the story. The full and unedited story.' Pauline's eyes never left Liam's the whole time she spoke. She wasn't concerned with the minor tremors on the sofa, it was only a grinning Laura settling herself in for the sorry tale about to be unleashed.

'Okay. So, about, seven – maybe eight months ago.'

'EIGHT MONTHS!'

They'd interrupted him as one with their shouts, but Pauline played the innocent party. When playfully slapping Laura's thigh and telling her to 'shush', she shifted any blame for the disruption away from herself. Laura had no chance to plead her case or to retaliate, Pauline was already cajoling Liam to continue.

'Okay,' Liam began again, albeit through an uneasy laugh. 'We were in company. And someone made a remark about a celebrity of sorts, somebody they thought should man-up and grow a pair. Well. I hate the man-up thing anyway, but I also questioned the validity of the other phrase.'

'About growing a pair of balls?' There was only one interrupting voice this time, and by walloping the slightly cringing Pauline with her stuffed cushion, Laura exacted her revenge. It was followed by an exaggerated order for her to, 'shush'.

'Yeah, that one,' wiping away his laughter at the girls goings-on, Liam composed himself to begin again. 'I remarked how tender the balls are, I mean It's not a secret right?' Glancing at one-another briefly to nod their heads in agreement, Laura and Pauline then turned their attention back to Liam. As one they implored him to continue. 'So, I remarked on the female genitalia.' Two heads that had been nodding involuntarily, stopped. 'I raised a point about those women who will occasionally scream out a request of, 'harder harder', to the man lying on top of them. So, you tell me – why is it that it's a pair of balls that signifies strength?'

When settling back into his chair Liam wondered why he was talking so much. And more to the point, the things he was talking about. He also wondered how long it would be before he'd be thrown out of the apartment and onto the street.

'A little risqué perhaps, but that's not so bad! And she finished with you for that? There must have been something else, surely?' Whilst Laura's words were a clue that she was unconvinced, her raised upper-lip was something else. Unless she was a fan of Elvis Presley, but there were no pictures of him on the wall.

'Balls,' Pauline interjected, with a delayed chuckle. 'Unless they were religious. Where they religious? I bet they were. As a woman, there's no middle ground with those lot. A virgin or a whore. Pick a side bitches, pick a side.'

'You pick a side, you witch,' laughed Laura. She again smacked Pauline with the cushion that up until then she'd held tight against her chest. So caught-up in Liam's story, she'd misinterpreted Pauline's words as a question. Or a slur.

The playful brawl that ensued with both parties battling hysterically for the outright control of fluffy soft furnishings, at least assured Liam he was safe from being kicked out onto the street. He was glad he'd opened-up. So-much-so, he interrupted what was turning out to be a rather one-sided contest. 'Yeah, you see,' he began again, before pausing to clear his throat and to make sure he had everyone's attention. He wanted to, felt he needed to confirm Laura's suspicions. 'Hands-up.' he began again after Laura conceded the cushion, and in turn defeat to a jubilant Pauline. 'Yeah. There was a little more to it. The company we were in – when I said those things. Well. We were around the dinner table on a Sunday afternoon. With her mum, dad and her little brother. We – she. She broke up with me the following day, by text message. And for the sake of full disclosure Pauline – yeah, devout C of E.'

Had Pauline's wide-open mouth been swearing there wasn't a chance it would have been heard over Laura's uproarious laughter. Liam wished he'd had the foresight to suggest to Pauline that six bottles of lager mightn't be enough for a proper night in, traditional or not. Another drink or two right now would be amazing. He'd made Laura laugh, and it was a genuine laugh too. Smiles can be easily faked by some people; but the secret is to look into their eyes. Those beautiful green eyes that lit up her face.

'Eight months though!' Pauline quizzed again. 'Aren't you looking for another girlfriend? Her glance to Laura as she asked the question was subliminally batted away. They both turned as one, again, to look at Liam.

'Not really, no.'

When asking, 'why?' Perhaps it was the way she'd asked it, but Laura seemed perplexed by her own question. And when trying to resettle herself into a comfortable position, Pauline wasn't for giving up her hard-won snuggly cushion. What she did get was another slap to her leg for her fidgeting. Pauline wanted Laura to hear the rest of Liam's story.

'To be honest, I'm bored with it all.'

'Bored?' Pauline and Laura asked in harmony.

'Yeah, bored of all the bullshit that comes with it. Those women who seem to be obsessed with wanting anyone and everyone to know how loved-up and apparently happy they are. Any casual day out must be transformed into a photo opportunity for social-media. It's all hashtag couple, hashtag love, hashtag this and that. Hashtag empty inside, if you ask me. Then they're kept busy by checking how many 'likes' and 'retweets' they get. I swear half of them are only doing it to try to attract an upgrade of sorts. Think about it, unhappy in their current relationship, but too insecure and afraid of being branded single, for those oh so shy girls it's less conspicuous than talking to a man in public. And better yet, for a certain class of lady, it's far less trashy than being on Tinder. God forbid. Hashtag desperate. I can't be bothered with any of that. If we were happy as a couple, truly happy, it wouldn't bother me if we were the only people on the planet who knew it. I want something different. I need something different.'

'Different how?'

It seems obvious, but how often do we all look back on things only to then think later, why didn't I - whatever? And when Pauline turned to see Laura's gaze transfixed on Liam, she knew she'd asked an excellent question. The obvious one. She also remembered how much she hated tennis, even Wimbledon. Caressing the back of her neck when turning to Liam again, she joined Laura in waiting for his answer.

'I'm.' As he paused to think about what he was about to divulge, Liam succeeded in nothing more than again wondering why he was opening-up to these women he barely knew. By this stage though he had little control of his thoughts and even less over his mouth, so on he went. 'I'm not trying to say – now, the thing is. You might think I'm trying to compare myself to – look. I'm just waiting. That's all.'

When looking to her friend when asking the next obvious question, 'waiting for what?' Pauline wasn't going to get any answers from Laura. Her attention was focussed exactly where it should have been, on Liam. Pauline clutched at her neck again when Liam let out a nervous laugh, before capitulating to elaborate, he went on, 'for my Yoko. Okay, that's it. I'm waiting for my Yoko Ono.'

'But the waiting?' Pauline was none the wiser. 'I get the Yoko Ono thing. I guess, kind of. But eight months – approximately! Rather than waiting, why don't you go out and find her. Your Yoko?'

Having already gone past the point of no return, well past it, Liam might as well tell them everything. Truth be told he couldn't shut himself up anyway.

'What should I do?' It was a rhetorical question, but Liam shuffled himself ready for a reply, just in case. None came.

'Should I trawl the bars and clubs to find an attractive woman who catches my eye? Should I approach her to start a conversation? I'd always maintain eye contact. I'd compliment her dress, her hair or her perfume. I'd make her laugh with one of my two cheeky jokes that I keep for such occasions. I could then hint at a bullshit story of my non-existent sporting prowess in either football or rugby. And trust me - within two minutes of meeting her I'd have worked out which sport would work best. Then I'd turn it up a notch with some saucy flattery to make her blush. And as soon as she stopped blushing to find the courage to look up from the floor, I'd be ready and waiting to compliment her rosy red cheeks. With eye contact.'

Pauline didn't want any popcorn, but her mouth was agape. Her hand was stuck fast in an almost empty bowl. Laura had sunk into her seat. Liam didn't have to ask, he knew he'd accurately described the life of a girl on a night-out and the one thousand approaches they deal with over a hundred different nights.

'To close the deal I'd compliment your beautiful eyes before lifting you into my strong arms to whisk you off to bed.' Liam's grand finale was complimented with an almost apologetic raising of his eyebrows. He was thankful though that neither of them had noticed he'd somewhat personalised his last sentence, by saying 'you', rather than 'her'. Not only was he immediately aware he'd said it, he wondered why. After once again double-checking that his bottles of lager were empty, they were, he reclined back into his chair with a smile. 'I've been there and done that. I'm bored now. I want something organic, not fabricated or forced. And If need be, I'll wait until she comes and finds me. My Yoko I mean, and I'm prepared to wait. Because I won't settle.'

Liam watched Pauline take her look from Laura to shift it onto her lap instead. As she stirred her hand around the almost empty bowl, Liam wondered what she was looking for. And Laura, well nothing. Her calm exterior perhaps belied an internal distress. Maybe Pauline could give her a hug.

An unexpected clearing of the throat from Laura took Liam's attention. Pauline's too, her neck cricked when she looked up.

'I don't make the rules,' Liam intervened, to disrupt what he assumed might be a backlash. In any event, by this point he was babbling through his own nerves.

'However, you do need to ask yourselves - as women. Does this happen because it's what you expect, or is it what you like? Men do all the chasing so to speak, and you women are the gatekeepers. As it stands your primary role in such matters seems only to be whether to say yes or no. In my humble opinion.' Despite the curious looks he was receiving from Laura, Liam kept on digging that hole.

'And please feel free to shoot me down.'

Which, when roughly translated could have been read as, 'please say something to stop me.' But no-one did. So again, on he went.

'Women already have all the power. The problem as I see it, is that most women have no idea how much power they have. And those that do, well. The vast majority of them are too afraid to use it. It is you, as women who have the power to decide what future generations will look and sound like.'

Liam had no-one to blame but himself, and he knew it. Idiot. Why hadn't he marched into that sitting-room and slumped himself down on the sofa next to Laura? It's a fact that the television in most households is the focal point of any room. With the television to his side and on stand-by, Liam was now the centre of attention. And with Pauline actively prodding Laura to put forward their side of the debate, he too was now on stand-by.

'One last thing,' Liam started again, he couldn't stop himself. 'Sorry. But just in case it's not clear, I'm all for equality. Although perhaps I'm having to pay a price for that. Personally I mean. But yeah, girl power.'

'Damn those bloody Spice Girls.'

Timidly lowering his raised and clenched fist of solidarity, Pauline's rapid and hostile response came as something of a surprise to Liam. The biting scowl that accompanied it was ferocious and If she'd spat on the floor too, that would have been less of a surprise. Liam wished he'd quit whilst he was ahead, if he ever was.

'They can't half chatter on Pauline, don't you think?'

'If you let them Laura. They're all the same really.'

Even though he knew he was being mocked, Liam smiled. He also knew where this was going next. He'd had the audacity to generalise about women and this would now be turned on him. He was outnumbered, it was two against one.

'I'm sorry, may I?' Laura's apology was deliberately insincere, if not sarcastic. Unravelling herself to sit on the edge of the sofa she went on with purpose. 'I mean, if it's okay. Can I? Do you mind?'

Laura's demeanour, whilst not entirely threatening strongly suggested she wasn't to be interrupted again. Not until she'd had her say. Never mind two against one, Liam didn't fancy his chances in a head-to-head.

'We, the both of us,' Laura began again, before turning to Pauline for confirmation that they spoke as one. The positive response from Pauline brought a lovely smile to Laura's face, momentarily. It dissipated as fast when she turned to face Liam again. 'Maybe we're selfish. But if anyone, and by anyone I do mean male or female ever tried to tell either of us what we could or couldn't do. Well, we're going to have issues. If I liked sports and dancing, and I wanted to be a cheerleader. Just you try and stop me. If I wanted to train to be an engineer, then I would. And I'd come top of my class too. And if I want to, as a single woman, enjoy an active and fulfilling sex-life – look. You get the general idea. The problem, our problem with girl power, and that shitty manufactured Spice Girls version of it is- '

'Damn those bloody Spice Girls.'

Laura was glad for Pauline's unscripted and sudden interruption. She didn't have any hang-ups about sex, not even her own sex life, but perhaps now wasn't the time. It was Pauline's go at it now.

'Women Liam.' Pauline began, after removing her hand from the sparse popcorn bowl to wag a finger and come to Laura's rescue. 'I'll give you the benefit of doubt and assume that you meant 'some women'. If you're having difficulty finding your Yoko, has it ever crossed your mind that you might be looking in the wrong places?' Reclining into the sofa, Pauline's wagging finger was also put to rest. And then she began again. 'Admittedly, at times we can be our own worst enemies. There are four billion of us and we're supposed to be individuals. If a woman doesn't want to do any of those things Laura mentioned, they shouldn't. As for the women who do. Well, the rest of us should learn to shut-up and let them enjoy themselves. To each their own and all power to them. There are some women who obsess in wanting every other woman on the planet to be just like them. Christ, what a boring world that would be. There are even some who rebel against being a woman, rather than revel in it. Now, it's usually those same women who will blame anyone and everything, other than themselves of course, for their own stupid insecurities and self-repression. They usually end up blaming the illuminati.

'Patriarchy, surely?' a pause from Pauline allowed Liam the opportunity to interrupt, with a valid point. 'You said, illuminati. But surely you mean, the patriarchy.'

'Ah, how right you are,' started Pauline again, as she sat forward in her chair with a smile. 'Isn't he a clever one?' There was no reply from Laura, she was as baffled as Liam. With a twinkle in her eye and an expanding grin that told Liam he'd probably been set-up, Pauline continued. 'I always get those imaginary foes mixed up.'

It was a trap. Pauline's sense of timing and, although he'd no idea where she was going with this, hopefully her comic banter, was spot-on. She'd obviously learnt a great deal from watching Laura's stand-up act. Although perhaps it was the other way around? Laura was sat captivated by Pauline, hanging on her every word. Then again, maybe it was a combination of both. You know what they say about teamwork.

'The blame game,' Pauline began again. 'Those who so delight in blaming others for their own weaknesses and failings. Or, as previously mentioned, their own self-repression. Name me any group of people who claim to be oppressed and hard done by. When you do, I'll give you a list of stinking rich and successful people within that group. Do you know why they're so successful? Because they go out and do it. Rather than sitting around to complain all the time they utilise their talents to get things done. As for the patriarchy - Well, my arse. When you can find the courage to talk to me about horny young girls running away from home to have babies in a war zone, because the males in their family-. Look, the thing is. There's not a lot of money to be made debating against any of these so-called ancient cultures or traditions.

Ultimately, we're all part of the same tribe. We are the ninety-nine percent of 'have-nots'. If you want something, go out and get it. Make it happen yourself, because nobody's going to hand it to you on a plate. Whilst losers fumble around looking for excuses and somebody else to blame, the winners are busy getting stuff done. Life is too short to be lived badly and on somebody else's terms. And as for the Spice Girls. The generation before us were fortunate enough to have role models and icons like Debbie Harry, Cyndi Lauper and Kate Bush. But we, my generation. We were supposed to build churches for, and fall at the feet of Sporty, Baby, Posh and – whoever those others were. Well, they can all fuck – right – off. To put it bluntly.

Ah, Debbie Harry. A glance again to the pictures on the wall answered something that had been bothering Liam since he'd first entered the sitting-room. He knew her name wasn't Blondie, but he couldn't for the life of him remember what it was. He also knew that one of the other Spice Girls was called Scary, which seemed ironic. He felt it best to keep that to himself, for the time-being.

'In my humble opinion,' Pauline began again. 'Unfortunately, feminism as we used to know it is dead. It's been hi-jacked by the middle-class and rather than concerning themselves with causes like an education for all women, worldwide. FGM. Or fighting to end forced marriages, otherwise known as legitimised rape. All they seem to be interested in are pay rises for themselves and a seat on the board of a big FTSE100 company. That's materialism, NOT feminism.

A contemplative and agreeing nod of Liam's head, combined with his thinking lips wasn't going to stop Pauline there.

'What's the difference between a middle-class millennial feminist and a capitalist with a vagina?' With no idea if he was being asked a question or told a joke, let alone the answer, Liam threw up his hands. 'I have no clue either,' Pauline taunted. 'Trickle-down doesn't work in economics and it won't work for feminism. Why do these so-called feminists think it will work for women? All women. They're big on words, but short on deeds.'

'You're so clever Pauline,' said Laura, before she turned to address Liam directly. 'Most of the women she speaks of, they have pieces of paper to prove how intelligent they are. Daddy bought them, from St Oxbridge's. I think the stupid hat things and the cloaks are optional though. How bizarre!'

'You're so funny Laura,' said Pauline. She smiled at her friend before her head then tilted gently to one side. 'And pretty too.'

As they drew themselves together to share a hug, Liam watched as Pauline and Laura's smiles came together as one. On withdrawing from their tender embrace it was evident Laura's cheek had momentarily attached itself and stuck to Pauline's. When disengaging from their clinch, it was like watching two opposing strips of Velcro being slowly stripped apart.

'I knew you'd been keeping all of the sweet popcorn for yourself,' shouted Laura. 'It's all over your face, you witch.'

'I did not, bitch.'

Had they pouted their lips they were close enough to kiss. However, from where Liam was sitting it didn't look or sound like there was going to be any male fantasy dream lesbian sex scene. Sitting eye to eye, nose to nose and chin to chin, Pauline and Laura shouted mild insults back-and-forth at each other. Within a matter of seconds though, and it could only have been the ferocity of their own laughter that blew them apart, in unison they turned again to look to Liam. They stared as one intently, and in anticipation. Okay, so Pauline licked the four fingers of one of her hands and was using them to wipe clean the side of her mouth. But still she waited, in anticipation.

'On a positive note.' On cue, Liam leant forward to speak again, whilst trying not to laugh and avoiding the obvious question of, 'what the fuck are you two like?' Turning to face Laura, as Pauline was already scavenging the bowl on her lap again, he continued. 'I agree with pretty much everything you've both said, but I don't think any of it contradicts my own thoughts on how ninety-nine percent of us find partners. And as a result, sorry for being selfish. But my own difficulties there-in.'

'Laura has a cond – Well, it's only because of this that she doesn't- '

'Doesn't agree with everything you've said.' Laura jumped in to halt Pauline in her tracks. She at the same time knocked the last half kernel of popcorn out from her wet and sticky fingers. 'You say you're bored, but we all have a type. What's yours?' Laura continued, whilst trying to ignore the disapproving looks from Pauline who lamented the last piece of popcorn, wondering where it had gone.

With his eyes closed to consider what his type was (he'd never given it much thought before), Liam surprised himself with what he said. Pauline too apparently. She adjourned her search down the back of the sofa.

'Comfortable, honest and strong.' So pleased was he with his reply to Laura's question, Liam took a spurt of confidence from it. 'You look confused Pauline.' They both did, but why pick a fight with the two of them? Pauline was a little put out by Liam's accusation, but even more so when she glanced across to see that Laura seemed to agree.

'Comfortable with where she's been and who she is now,' Liam began again. 'We all have a past, of course we do. But that's where it should stay, it shouldn't be allowed to influence the present or our futures. As for honest. If she was unhappy about something, then talk to me about it. Trust me, in every sense. I don't understand why people say you can only gain certain levels of trust after being together for – well however many years - why? Now, even more pertinent perhaps- '

'Pertinent.' Whether she was taking her revenge for his 'confused' jibe, or couldn't contain her excitement, Pauline interrupted Liam to shout out. It probably was just excitement, as she then carried on. 'Nine letters. An adjective. Relating directly to the matter at hand.' A reminder from Laura that there was a lost kernel of popcorn somewhere, accompanied with a whack to her arm brought Pauline's mind back into focus. 'Sorry, sorry.'

'More pertinent perhaps,' laughed Liam. 'Strong. If she portrays herself as a strong woman, that's great. But she shouldn't go on to expose herself later as a phoney. Talk to me about your likes, hates, fears, hopes, dreams and ambitions. Anything. And perhaps most importantly. If she does like me, she'll let me know. Laughing at my shitty jokes and playing with her hair, well, that doesn't do it for me. I'm not expecting to be approached by someone who's going to say, hi. I'm your Yoko, do you fancy a shag? But for Christ's sake, let me know.'

Laura was almost as happy as Pauline when she saw her hold aloft the rogue piece of popcorn. Whilst listening to Liam she'd managed to rescue it by blindly fumbling around the back of the sofa. Had it not been found now it would only have found its way stuck onto someone's clothes a week later. There were more important matters at hand though. 'That's all very well,' Laura began. 'But don't you think there's a chance that you might, subconsciously- '

'Oh. Subconsciously. Another adject – ouch.' Another thump from Laura had Pauline ducking for cover. She swirled her hand around an empty bowl. 'Sorry – sorry – sorry.'

'Deep down.' Laura's glance toward Pauline as she began again reminded her of a puppy she'd had as a kid. The one that was forever pissing on the carpet. In stark contrast Liam could barely contain himself, until Laura turned to look at him to go on again. 'Deep down, don't you think there's a chance you could miss out on something? Or someone, who might be perfect for you? Something right in front of your face even. Because essentially, you've stopped looking.'

Even from side-on as she stared at Laura, Pauline's eyes looked like they'd been propped open with matchsticks. Although Laura sat suddenly rigid, her eyes darted every which way. Every which way other than toward Liam or Pauline.

'You still look confused.' Liam addressed Pauline, as Laura clearly had other things going on. 'Maybe even more so now,' he chuckled. 'It's simple really. I'm putting all my trust in my granny. She pretty much lives her life by the old saying of, whatever will be, will be. You know. Que sera, sera.'

'Not wanting to be anal,' Pauline came back with. 'But I'd plump for perplexed, rather than confused.' A look to Laura to see her somewhat agitated and stuck for words gave her the all-clear to continue. 'I'm not going to lie, I was expecting him to say the usual stuff. You know - blonde hair and a decent pair of tits.' On turning away from a grinning again Laura to face Liam, she went further still. 'It sounds to me like you might be looking for a dirty girl.'

Throwing her hands up and in front of her mouth that was as wide-open as her eyes, Laura relented to shout out, 'O. M. Fucking G. Pauline. In the last ten minutes you've said the words balls, vagina, whores, tits and anal. Out loud. You're a potty mouth.' She'd have words with her later, meantime, girls swearing freely in front of boys was always a good distraction technique.

'I know!' screamed Pauline, when she mimicked Laura's hand onto mouth look, whilst at the same time fanning frantically her free hand up and down in front of her face to simulate comedic timidity. 'And in front of a boy too,' she squealed. All three of them burst into a synchronised fit of hilarity, but when Pauline and Laura rolled over each other on the sofa, Liam was on his own.

'Liam said he wants to write with me.'

'That's not what I- '

'Write a book together,' Pauline cut short Liam's faint protest. 'I'll help. We'll have to use some of the big words like rhapsodic, tumescent and equivocal.'

'Pauline! Are those nine letter words? Have you been binge watching Countdown again?'

'Define binge?' Pauline's guilty smile was followed by a guilty frown and raised hands of guilt.

Liam thought about conveying the point that he'd wanted someone to read his work, rather than working together, but he'd said enough already. Besides, he was nowhere near ready to do anything with Laura. Yet.

'I wish you the best of luck in waiting for a girl to come and find you,' started Laura. 'And whilst tonight has been exquisite,' she paused to look at Pauline with a smile after finding her own nine letter word. 'I'm off to bed.'

In a single movement Laura jumped up from the sofa and onto her feet. She was a little surprised when directly across from her, Liam followed suit.

'I'm not – I didn't think – It's a manners thing.' Liam tried to swat away the contrasting looks of suspicion from Laura, and those of glee from Pauline. 'I can't catch a break,' he finished tamely, as Laura made her way to the sitting-room door.

'I have a vibrator in my bedside cabinet and a baseball bat under my bed. I only want to use one of them tonight, don't force my hand.' Having turned to make her way into the hall, Laura about turned as quickly to pop her head back through the open doorway. 'Pun intended,' she smirked, before departing again.

The sound of Laura's bedroom door closing signalled a minute of awkward silence as Liam tried to summon the courage to look again at Pauline. Ultimately, he had no choice, he could feel her eyes burning straight through him.

'Are you going through?' The look on Pauline's face as she waited for Liam's reply was akin to a punter with ringside tickets for the big fight, or someone with front-row seats for the latest must-see premiere in the West-End. Liam couldn't decide which.

'I thought she was the comedian.'

'Hang in there,' said Pauline, when she came back with a smile and raised eyebrows. 'You know,' she smiled some more without looking up. 'She likes you.'

'What makes you think that? I saw no evidence- '

'If she didn't like you, she'd already be sitting on – Look, girls talk. We know stuff.'

'Girls talk. Yes. To each other, but not – oh never mind, I've gotten myself into enough bother alrea. ---- Hang on a minute. You don't like the salty popcorn either, do you? So why the hell- '

'It's tradition,' said Pauline, but the finger she pressed onto her lips couldn't hide her rowdy smile. 'Tonight was fun. I bet you're glad you came.' There was no popcorn left and Pauline knew it, but she stared down into the empty bowl anyway. 'Maybe you could bring your friend with you - next time.'

'Hah, your friend!' Liam laughed. 'Look at you, pretending you're all shy.' After replicating Pauline's own playful accusation from earlier, he then went on again, only with an insightful grin now. 'I think now might be a good time to tell you. Graeme has been on Countdown, the TV show.'

Pauline's elongated and impassioned response contained more vowels than were technically allowed.

'Oh yes. And guess what? Not only has he appeared on Countdown, he has two very ugly teapots to prove it.'

Pauline knew the significance of a Countdown teapot. Graeme was a champion, a two-time champion. As she threw herself back to lay down flat on the sofa, her hands gripped tight into and pulled against her top as she howled with enthusiasm. Thinking it prudent to make his exit now, Liam made his way down the hall and hoped that Pauline's wailing would drown out the sound of any battery-operated toys. He then thought it wise to get out of the front-door sharpish too. Pauline's ongoing hollering could annoy Laura to such an extent she might burst out of her room swinging a baseball bat.

On closing the door behind him, Liam tried to recall some of the things Pauline had said to him. He hoped two bottles of lager were enough to have her tipsy and talkative, as opposed to drunk and delirious.

11

Can you imagine having to deal with a different next-door neighbour every year? A huge number of businesses on Tenerife go bust every season. It's fair to say there are times when some cocky Brit has assumed that to buy a little café or a pub out here was a license to print money. Maybe they hadn't put in the research to see how many other English-speaking businesses they would be in competition with. Some of them also think they're coming out here on holiday, and in-turn they become a little too fond of the sunbathing and cheap booze.

To not only survive but to be successful in this game you must have your own style and your own patter. You must stand out from the crowd and be an individual. The trick is, whenever you get a punter through the door you have to make them want to come back. If you get a family of five or six people in on the first day of their holiday, and then get them to come back consistently over the next fourteen days (and nights if possible) that's the secret. It is possible, and if you can repeat that formula from the month of April through to August, then Bob would indeed be your uncle and his gorgeous wife was called Fanny.

There are hundreds of books and thousands of online courses that offer up the secrets to running a successful business, and some of them specialise in how to do this abroad. They share their in-depth formulas and explanations for everything and everyone to help you succeed. Ultimately though, you've either got it or you haven't.

'Morning lads. Including you, I suppose. Prick.'

Having watched the smiling Laura approach, Liam's rapture was tempered somewhat by an injury she seemed to be carrying. She walked with a slight limp, which Liam associated as something akin to a groin strain he'd once suffered whilst playing football. Perhaps she'd overdone it with her sex-toy the previous evening. Regardless of the deep conversations they'd shared the night before, he didn't know her well enough to bring this up in company. Besides, she was already in full flow herself. She was having a go at his idiot of a mate.

'That's fine. I probably deserve that.'

With her pencil and pad already in hand, Laura stood poised to scribble 'shock' and 'horror'. When she looked first to Liam and then Graeme, she received only smiles in return and absolutely no help in deciphering what was going on.

'I've been an arsehole. I know that now, and I'd like to apologise. I'm sorry.'

With Laura unable to speak, Graeme thought he should help by filling in some of the blanks. Although he did begin by blithely chiding Laura and Liam for not letting him know about the movie night he'd missed out on. Liam took the look he got from Laura as one that had 'snitch' written large on it. No translators were required.

Their mate, after disappearing the previous day, had apparently met someone on the beach. And the reason he couldn't be found was because he'd stayed there all night. He'd spent the whole night 'just talking' with this new-found friend. Notwithstanding, as well as Liam giving up on his search for a movie night, it was debatable how long Graeme had spent looking. When returning to their hotel after leaving Laura and Pauline's, Liam had been greeted by the sound of a snoring Graeme. When he'd given him a shake to ask what had happened, he was rewarded with a friendly 'fuck-off', accompanied by a lager scented burp.

'What's her name? We should erect a statue in her honour.'

The silence that followed Laura's question allowed Graeme and Liam the time to wait for an answer too, but none came. With his mates head bowed to cover his new-found and quite welcome modesty, Liam thought he would be the good guy and relieve some of the pressure. After-all, even after everything, they were still pals. 'He hasn't told us anything either. Won't say a thing, but hey. That's cool. I mean- '

'Yeah, I know. I was only teasing, or testing.' Laura interrupted. 'I said the word *erect,* and he never batted an eye. He's cured I tell you. It's a fucking miracle.'

When the laughter ended and an order of two fried breakfasts had been placed (only Graeme and Liam were staying to eat), Laura was asked if she and her friend had any plans for this evening. She needn't have looked up from her pad to know who'd asked the question as old habits die hard, and once a player always a player. When looking at all three of the guys (two of them had buried their heads), Laura wondered why the other was grinning from ear to ear whilst rubbing at a fresh bruise appearing on his shin. 'I've heard there's an eighties club called Tropicana that isn't bad,' he laughed, as he glanced to Graeme on his right and then Liam on his left. When pulling his legs in close together again, he used his hands to protect his shins. 'Do you know it?'

With Graeme raising his head to look around or through her and toward the café, whilst trying not to make it look comically obvious, Laura took pity. There was the small matter of Pauline saying she'd liked him, and she hadn't danced once today. She could probably use a decent night out with some proper company.

'Do I know Tropicana? You know I live here?'

Remembering the previous interaction between Graeme and Pauline, Laura was already on-board with this idea, but she had no intention of making it easy. On top of everything she was lapping it up that Liam was plausibly afraid to raise his head. When focusing in on Graeme, and then deliberately stepping in front of his eyeline to get his attention, she quizzed what he was looking for. And whatever it was - she said, 'you won't find it between my legs.' As Graeme managed to mumble out an embarrassed reply of sorts, to suggest he had no idea what she was talking about, Liam found the strength to lift his head. And then some more to open his mouth and save his mate.

'So, anyway. Tropicana?'

'Yeah, it's decent I suppose. I used to know the DJ.' Laura began with a telling smile. 'Pauline likes it far more than me though. Tell you what, I might talk to her about that. Anyway, I'll go and get these breakfasts.' Laura turned from the table there and then as she didn't want to break out a laugh in front of Liam, or the others. To have done that might have ruined her next little wind-up. 'Ah,' she began with a longing sigh. 'I haven't seen Mickey in a while. It'll give us a chance to catch-up again. I wonder how he's doing,' she said out loud, whilst walking away.

Quite unsure of the reason behind the muffled sniggers from the departing Laura, Liam was just glad he hadn't embarrassed himself with any foolish comments. He'd judged that any ill-advised and incriminating comments about her use of sex-toys adversely affecting her gait might have caused some embarrassment. Besides, even in her loose-fitting skirt that now swayed back and forth elegantly, it was noticeable how she walked today with a satisfactory spring in her step. Even though Laura was getting smaller and smaller as she walked away (elementary science), she still managed for the most part to annoy Graeme by covering his view to the cafes window. Regardless of how far he leant across onto the edge of his seat, or any angle he tried to exploit, he couldn't see anything of any note. Nothing. 'Unbelievable!'

Graeme and Liam's minds were brought back into focus with a dead leg each in quick succession. After being questioned why they'd had such difficulty in having this romantic date planned for them, they were then condemned for their probable lack of any testicles. A warning endorsed with raised hands and an oscillating head that no more help would be forthcoming, alongside another invitation to 'grow a pair', was their departing friends closing statement to a pair of absorbed and distracted lost boys.

'Guess who's come back, and trying to summon the courage to ask us – What the fuuuu- '

Pauline didn't have to guess or be told who'd returned to the café. She knew full well who was sitting outside as she'd been standing at the window manically waving out into the courtyard, trying to get some attention. After cursing her pal for constantly blocking her view (Laura seemed to have an unbelievable knack for doing this), Pauline had retreated to her kitchen. Manning her cooker by the time Laura returned, not even her deranged grin could deflect attention from the little button mushroom she pressed hard against her crotch, bulbous end out. 'Would Mr Trump like mushrooms with his breakfast?' she laughed.

With an exhale of breath that curled her lips, and a groan to suggest the sight of Pauline's imitation penis was going to make her puke, Laura grabbed the mushroom to throw it in the bin. She was in the process of beginning to explain how the orange 'Donald' one seemed to have turned a corner. She was going to explain that he'd met someone and become a better man for it. She was going to, but she didn't. Pauline wasn't in the least bit interested in anything Laura had to say on the matter. If her dancing up and down the length of the kitchen was any clue, she had other things on her mind. Far better things. The only thing better than a night on the tiles for Pauline, was a day at work spent dancing on them. She did then stop suddenly, mid-spin to enquire, 'did the Graeme one ask after me? Did he?'

12

Wearing his new pair of trainers bought especially for this holiday, his favourite pair of jeans and a designer polo shirt so new he'd forgotten to iron out its creases, Graeme was at last content with how he looked. He hadn't asked Liam for his 'honest' opinion for ten minutes. They'd gotten ready far too early so decided there'd be no harm in having a quick 'livener' before meeting the girls. A bit of Dutch courage would relax the nerves and loosen the tongue, just enough. He hadn't said anything, but Liam also hoped the additional time might allow the fresh air to partially neutralise Graeme's fragrance. It was a decent aftershave, but perhaps that was the issue. Rather than dabbing on a little of his everyday potion, he'd gone to town with his 'tonight's the night'.

With the minor debate over how they'd managed to facilitate this evening at an end (Laura had come out to clear their breakfast plates and was so busy she'd said only three words. Tropicana, tonight, seven) Liam and Graeme took in some of the sights on the strip. They were glad it was just the two of them and they didn't have to babysit a drunk. It was official, the holiday starts now.

Indulging in the ongoing shenanigans on the main-strip wasn't going to make the lads late for their impending date, not even when they'd stopped briefly to lark around with a crowd of blokes dressed up as Santa's. Liam and Graeme played wingmen when they told of the horny Hen Party who'd accosted them not ten minutes past. On this island, tonight at least, those two parties would be a match made in heaven.

'You're early. How refreshing?'

When eventually ambling into the Tropicana, Liam and Graeme were surprised to see Pauline and Laura holding cocktails against their smiling lips. It was Liam who was most taken aback, and him who'd shouted out his obvious shock. He and Graeme were fifteen minutes early themselves. He remembered again, when double-checking his watch, that he'd adjusted time zones well in advance. Before leaving for the airport he'd managed to convince Graeme, when he'd turned up at his house two hours early, that he didn't want to get caught-up in traffic and was excited for the holiday.

'Early!' Pauline shouted back gleefully, 'we've been here for at least half an – about ten minutes.' A subtle nudge and a sideways glance from Laura brought Pauline's own wristwatch into view. It also offered an opportunity for her to re-evaluate how long they'd been waiting, or what she should and shouldn't divulge.

'Refreshing?' quizzed Laura, to cover for Pauline's overly exuberant honesty. 'Did you expect - or want us to turn up fashionably late? If it's clichés you're after, then I suggest – we suggest you look elsewhere.' With a straw held loosely between her smiling lips, Pauline's eyes spoke a thousand words, and not one of those words would be of any use to Laura in starting a meaningless debate. Laura was given no opportunity anyway, following Liam's carefree rebuttal of, 'yeah, okay. Fair point.'

'You look amazing,' Graeme shouted out without thinking, before slotting easily into place next to Pauline. Again, without thinking. Laura wanted to question him on his lack of manners, when he hadn't acknowledged her presence. She didn't bother, when realising he probably wouldn't have heard her anyway. He had eyes for one person only and couldn't have told you if anyone else was present.

'I just threw these on. But thank-you. You look all shiny and new.' Pauline smiled when she leant forward to reach out her hand, wanting to touch the sleeve of Graeme's sparkling white polo shirt. He couldn't be certain if it was him who'd moved or not, but Pauline's hand didn't make it onto his arm. As she held her straw firm for a nervous sip, Pauline hoped Laura and Liam would start talking to each other soon. They would surely then take their beady eyes off her, and Graeme.

Standing back to admire the exchanges between their friends, Laura and Liam understood why they were here this evening. Glancing back and forth between Graeme and Pauline's silliness and each other, there was no point in either of them butting in. You must be careful when dealing with electricity. Without realising it, Pauline and Graeme were in the process of giving over little pieces of themselves to each other.

When Liam's look returned to Laura, her smile grew wider. It was a toss-up whether she was enjoying the charming dialogue between their friends or Liam's silence. Liam also found the different body language interesting. Whilst Pauline leant forward and into Graeme, to engage in what looked like a riveting conversation, Laura leant back casually with one of her arms laid flat on the bar. There was no point waiting for Laura to speak. She wasn't just content with the silence, she was soaking it up. Almost radiant with joy. To continually and indiscriminately survey the bar would only make Liam look more of a fool than he already was, but If he dared glance toward Graeme again, and was caught doing so, what a simpleton he'd feel for his own stupid awkwardness. He'd spoken to countless girls, and never had any real difficulty doing-so. But this was somehow different. This all seemed very new.

Unable to see the spectres of past disappointments that sat on his shoulders to whisper in his ear, Liam looked to the floor beneath his feet.

A gentle kick at an imaginary football brought with it a goal into the top corner. Surely, if there was a time to question Laura on her sore leg, and an opportunity to sidle in some saucy little jokes about her possible over-use of sex-toys, then this was it. Between slurps of her cocktail (she'd discarded her straw), Laura continued to almost mockingly grin at Liam's interminable discomfort. Unlike Liam, she wasn't for shying away from eye contact. Strained though he was, Laura's sore leg and her use of sex-toys was a discussion just waiting to be exploited. This was Liam's ace card and would be used as a funny ice-breaking conversation opener. 'So, the eighties then.' A last second change of heart with the intention being to ease his way into things later (obviously), would be a better plan of attack. 'How come the two of you are so into that decade? I know where he gets it from.'

Staring blankly at the bar counter and the tacky ice-bucket sat on there, Liam wanted to punch it. Modelled on a pineapple it was tacky and annoying, but not the primary cause of his outrage. Facing an open goal he'd miskicked his shot well over the bar and into the empty stands behind. It could have been this sudden outburst that reminded Graeme and Pauline they weren't alone, but it was more likely to have been the clenched fist of Liam's outstretched arm that had connected with Graeme's shoulder. With Pauline palpably incensed at this unnecessary and abrupt interruption, Liam found no solace from Graeme either. Now probably wasn't the time to mention they already looked like an old married couple.

Liam had in the past had some proper dodgy looks from his mate, but nothing like this one. Imagining himself to be under the blazing hot sun in the African trenches with Michael Caine in the Zulu film, Liam reached out slowly for his pint of lager. It was a bucket of water he needed. Ice-cold water.

'My dad,' Laura managed to spit out, without losing any of her drink through her nose. She'd been taking a sip when Liam's unease had called on him to interrupt Graeme. 'My dad introduced us to the music and movies from the eighties,' she went on. After a gentle rub of her nostrils and a check for any spillage onto her crew-neck cashmere sweater (it was only the second time she'd taken it out of her closet), she then offered a carefully concealed and mouthed apology to Pauline.

'Brainwashed you mean,' proposed Pauline.

Allowing his shoulders to drop into their rightful place and his lungs to be filled with fresh oxygen, Liam would go down the comedy road with his conversation. He couldn't go down the sex-toy route now anyway, not now that Graeme was listening. He'd save that for later. Maybe. 'So, you're a daddy's girl?'

From the corner of an eye Liam saw Pauline's hand urging Graeme into action. With Graeme having no idea what he was supposed to do, a shrug of his shoulders was all he could manage. Internally cursing the fallacy that everyone, absolutely everyone from his part of the world was supposedly gifted with a funny gene, Liam waited for the confirmation of his latest transgression. He began to think that, from this point on, it might be best for him to keep his humour to himself. He didn't have to wait too long.

'Our mum abandoned us when we were little kiddies, so yeah. I suppose I probably could be considered a bit of a daddy's girl.'

FUCK! Liam scalded himself inwardly.

'Abandoned is a bit harsh, and he wasn't to know.' Pauline's attempt to appease the situation halted any apology from Liam, but it did also divert attention from his silently screaming facial expression. Liam was going to have to think on his feet when it was clear he'd be receiving no further help. Pauline was already explaining to Graeme what had happened, using only her eyes.

'I'm sorry.' An apology from Laura came quickly and was contrite. It also proved beyond doubt how close she and Pauline were. 'Okay. But I don't have any issues with being a daddy's girl, because it's not what you're imagining.' Laura began to authenticate. 'I was never dressed in pink ribbons or sent to ballet classes. And when he sat me down on his knee to tell me a story, it wasn't about make-believe Princesses who would grow up to meet and marry a wanky Prince. He told me stories of his own childhood heroes.'

'Lennon and McCartney,' Liam tendered softly. This was a guess that couldn't and surely wouldn't bring him any trouble, or unwanted attention. Amen to the Beatles. Surely?

'Souness and Dalglish.' Graeme countered in a flash. He loved a competitive quiz.

'Derek Hatton and Arthur Scargill.' A glance at the two lads with an audible sigh, confirmed what Laura would normally expect when telling this anecdote. Vacant and faraway looks. It was far from the most exciting of stories to tell, Socialism just isn't sexy anymore.

'Google them,' laughed Pauline. 'And read up on your bloody history.' Physical contact was at last made when she placed her hand gently onto Graeme's chest. 'I expect better from you,' she smiled when giving a tender rub, before withdrawing again with a blush.

'You said us, a minute back. Sorry to bring it up again.' It was only a roundabout apology but better than trying to bury his head in the sand to duck out of an already half-asked, or half-arsed question. 'How many brothers and sisters do you have? I'm going to take a stab at a few big brothers. You're tough.' It wasn't a typical compliment to pay a girl, but Liam thought it spot on for Laura. And one she'd hopefully relate to. 'I imagine because you grew up in a house full of older boys, you've had to constantly stand your ground and fight your corner.' A supplementary compliment about her strength of character would make up for his earlier clanger.

Stopping short of rubbing his fingernails against his chest in triumph when Laura confirmed she had three brothers, Liam's exultant smirk was clear enough for everyone to see anyway. Until Laura wiped it from his face. 'Younger brothers, all of them. If I am tough, if. Then they're not getting any of the credit for it.'

The smile beginning to break across Liam's face showed he understood Laura's subtle hint. She, as a woman, was unafraid of being characterised as 'tough'. On finally managing to hit a bullseye and now in full-swing, the obvious next step was to ask the names of her three brothers.

FUCK! Another silent scream followed Laura's announcement of the names of her siblings. It was also clear why she'd felt the need to let out another audible and exasperated sigh before doing so.

'Fuck off,' laughed Graeme, who up until that point had felt it best to stay silent and well clear of any trouble. A slap on his shoulder from Pauline, and a stare that could fell goats was confirmation that he should have listened to his instincts. Or not use a swear word, he wasn't sure which.

Laura confirmed her brothers names again, slowly. 'John, Paul and George. 'I'm not bullshitting. Those are their names.'

Liam cursed internally again. Why didn't he go for the footballers? He'd had first pick at it too. Idiot. Was there nothing he could do right with this girl? Unless? Her dad must have been a big fan though, of the Beatles. Otherwise, why would he have chosen, or allowed them to be called those names? Get in! Result. Even a blind man can hit a bullseye eventually, if you give him enough darts.

'Or Sooty,' Pauline said aloud. She was so pre-occupied at the time in soothing Graeme's sore shoulder, she hadn't realised she'd spoken out loud. 'What?' she asked, when looking up and into Graeme's eyes to see him staring down quizzically. Liam's wary gaze then drew her onto the dubious and disbelieving Laura. 'Oh right, Sooty. Can I tell them? Can I?'

Barely waiting for the conciliatory nod from Laura to give her the go-ahead to tell her story, Pauline's hands had been set in motion for added drama and effect.

The youngest of Laura's three brothers had been feeling unwell for a couple of days and, with no sign of any recovery imminent, a doctor was called for a home visit. The doctor's prognosis wasn't positive, so an ambulance was called to take little George to the hospital. As he was only eleven years old at the time and in need of adult supervision, Laura went with him. For additional support, Pauline went too. On reaching the hospital little George was taken into a private booth to be checked over by yet another doctor. Whilst Laura stayed with him, Pauline waited on the other side of the drawn screens. When stopping for a moment to settle her shaking hands and to take another sip from her straw, Pauline could see that her fervour in relaying this story wasn't being matched by Laura. As well as being present at the time of this incident, Laura had heard Pauline tell this story before, although she'd struggle to recall her ever being so animated when doing so.

'And then.' After an almost repentant shrug of her shoulders, Pauline continued. 'All I could hear from behind the screens was little George screaming at the top of his voice. He was shouting, "his hands up my bum. He's got his hand up my bum."'

'It was confirmed as appendicitis. They had to operate on him that night.' Laura halted the half-laughter come shock from Liam and Graeme. Particularly Liam, knowing he'd have to be extra vigilant in watching his every step. 'He got through it though, thankfully,' Laura confirmed, with a narrowing of her eyes toward her friend.

'Sooty though. Do you get it? He got through it, but he'll never get over it.' Pauline smiled as she crossed her arms across her chest to give a pseudo hug to her absent little friend. 'Oh, the wee sweetie. He knows I adore him.' Her raised head and a smile to match more than advertised Pauline's feelings toward little Sooty - George.

'That wee sweetie is now six-foot-three inches tall and a regional Judo champion,' said Laura, whose raised eyebrows were also joined by her smile. 'Just saying,' she concluded with a nodding head, and no shortage of pride.

'What about- '

Managing to stop himself in the nick of time, and before any more blunders were made, Liam couldn't fathom whether Laura's squinting eyes were quizzical or suspicious. She'd every right to be suspicious. What he'd stopped himself from asking, was why there was no Ringo.

Remembering Laura had been abandoned by her mother when she was a child, that's why there was no Ringo. Idiot.

Perhaps that was why her mother had left home, because she didn't want to take the chance of giving birth to another boy? Ringo Starr always got a bad rap, poor Ringo. With comedy clearly not his strongpoint, and no sense of timing, Liam dug himself out of a half-dug hole when turning away from Laura's prying eyes. 'What about you Pauline? I assume the both of you got into this eighties stuff together?'

'Well yeah, pretty much.'

What an escape. Unbeknown to anyone else Liam's nodding head and luminous grin were more of a self-congratulatory pat on his back, rather than any delight in Pauline's confirmation. A half-turn when combined with his half-smile should have demonstrated to Laura, she had nothing to worry about. This was where he'd been going with his question all along.

'During the summer holidays one year, between leaving primary school and going to secondary,' Pauline began to give more detail. 'I had a sleepover at Laura's house-'

'And she never left.' Laura laughed out loud when interrupting. She laughed some more when Pauline spilt some of her drink when jumping across to give her a hug.

'It's true,' said an emotional Pauline. When stepping back to be once again at Graeme's side, she'd given him a smile and a wink when placing her hand on his arm to gently edge herself in. 'She won't say it out loud,' she continued. 'But I know she loves me. We come as a team.'

It was unusual to hear of a woman leaving the family home, and rarer yet for her to leave the kids. There are many reasons why families fall apart, and who knows what goes on behind the closed curtains of any house to make anyone leave, male or female? But to have done it the summer before your eldest daughter was about to start at a new school! There was no way he was going to ask for confirmation, but this was what Liam took from Pauline's very public show of emotion.

'I wasn't mistreated at home or anything,' Pauline began to explain her side of the story. 'I wasn't their main priority is all. They're divorced now, my mum and dad. But we still go to my mums house anytime we're back home. This one though.' When Pauline pointed at her, Laura sipped incessantly on her fruity drink. She was cowering away from Pauline's poking finger, but her emotions too. Pauline went on regardless. 'She might come across as a bit of a mouthy so-and-so at times, but she needs someone to look after her.'

The laughter that broke out caused the last remnants of Laura's cocktail to be spilt. Or spit, depending on your perspective. Graeme felt at this point he had no option but to join in with his own sorry tale. 'I'm a mistake, if anyone's interested.'

When Laura crouched up and turned to one side, whilst at the same time lifting a defensive knee to protect herself from Liam's wayward spittle, she needn't have worried. The little lager that did escape from his mouth was sprayed onto the hand he'd thrown up in front of it. He was a better goalkeeper than a centre-forward. He knew Graeme's story back to front but was a little surprised to be on the verge of hearing it again now. On a positive note though, rather than receiving a telling off from Laura for almost spraying her in a shower of second-hand lager, her laughter was as entrancing as it was hysterical.

'Why I like eighties music,' Graeme went on. 'I have a brother and a sister who are both more than twenty years older than me. I was brought up with that music playing in my house every day.'

'Twenty years! Really?' Laura looked first to Graeme when asking the question, and then to Liam for confirmation. She got it in spades when, like those little nodding dogs in the backs of cars, they responded together. Oh, yes, yes, yes.

'Honestly.' Graeme ceased his nodding to augment his story with more detail. 'Back home, there's a Geography teacher who calls me uncle Graeme.' As the laughter began to subside, Graeme placed the cherry on top. 'He's two years older than me and has a big bushy beard. But to him, I'm his uncle Graeme!'

When all eyes then somehow fell naturally onto Liam, whether it was a want or a need to open-up or just peer group pressure, he told his own tale of so-called dysfunctionality. His parents immigrated to Canada when he was fifteen years old. And at the time, because he didn't want to go, he'd put his foot down and was allowed to stay behind with his granny. 'I hate the cold weather, and their national sport is Ice-hockey.' Liam grimaced with a shake. 'And besides, can you imagine being in one of those oddball nuclear families? One with a married mum and dad and two-point-two kids. I mean, weirdo's!'

'Whatever will be, will be.' said Laura under her breath, and not loud enough for anyone to hear.

Knowing smiles and agreeing heads were followed by a brief period of silence, although it didn't seem to bother anyone too much. They were so comfortable in each-others company, no-one felt any need or pressure to spoil the quiet with irritating and mindless small-talk.

Oblivious to anything or anyone around her now, Pauline saw only Graeme. She hadn't a care if anyone was watching as she placed gently her hand onto his shoulder. She rubbed gently again where she'd earlier landed a blow. It hadn't hurt then and wasn't sore now, but Graeme wasn't one for complaining. Her soothing hand moved down from his shoulder and onto his bare arm, and from there it slid slowly down again to cup his elbow into the palm of her warm and open hand. It was the most basic of skin on skin contact, akin only to a friendly handshake perhaps, but to Graeme it felt like so much more. Holding his pint glass in his other hand, if his strong but shaky grip on it didn't cause it to shatter, he might just work up a frothy head onto it.

'I need to piss,' announced Pauline, before turning to place her glass down onto the bar. On turning around again her smile suggested she more than likely needed to pee out of excitement. As she breezed between Laura and Liam, causing him to take a step back, Liam thought better of asking Graeme how things were going. He hadn't even bothered to wait for Pauline to disappear before slumping himself forward and down onto the bar. If he did have any words, he wasn't in any fit state to share them. It was as if someone had stuck a pin in him, causing him to deflate. He was as flat as his half-drunk pint of lager.

Staring at the pint glass he'd managed to place on the bar counter, only just saving himself from dropping it, Graeme was reminded that it was that cheap Spanish crap you say you won't buy but always do. When his head then dropped into his arms, he wondered why his legs were jutting back and forth with no rhyme or reason.

Left to his own devices and still unsure where to begin any meaningful discussion with Laura, Liam tried to buy himself some thinking time by asking why Laura wasn't going to the toilet with Pauline.

'More clichés! You really are going to have to do much better.'

At some ease, because Laura's put down was done with a grin, Liam then asked her a question on her general wellbeing. When asking her about her leg, he asked if she'd had an accident. He made no mention of any sex-toys though, he could save that for later. Maybe?

'It was the weather. Sometimes the weather has an adverse effect on me.'

'It must have been thirty-degrees!'

'I thought you wanted to talk about your writing.' Laura almost barked back at him when raising her head, and at the same time a new and completely unrelated topic.

With Graeme's head slumped into his arms and in no fit state for, well anything really, Liam's secret passion for writing was still safe.

Impotent – It probably isn't the best choice of word to use when describing a man's prowess in any given field. Powerless. Yes. Almost powerless as he stood in front of this girl with her golden hair and eyes the colour of a passionate and furious green sea that could sink any ship, Liam wondered why no-one wrote songs about such things. He knew the song about the brown eyed girl, everyone does. And although he couldn't think of any off the top of his head, there were probably hundreds about blue-eyed boys and girls.

Abandoned by her friend to be left with two guys at the bar (although a quick glance to Graeme showed him to be incapacitated through emotion), Laura waited. She waited for Liam to fall into line with the usual bullshit that was used to try and charm her out of her knickers. Maybe it wouldn't be the worst thing that had ever happened, she thought. She watched with fascination Liam's clumsy attempts to camouflage his trepidation with aloofness. When she looked into his eyes, that were initially looking into her own, she then followed them all around the room. She wouldn't tease him anymore. She would leave him in peace for a while, to compose himself. She decided to wait. So she waited - and waited....

'I don't think I've ever met anyone quite like you before,' Liam eventually opened with. 'And I really- '

'Shit!'

It wasn't the response Liam had been looking for or expecting, and it took him back a little. And then he let Laura's eyes guide his own. Together they watched a group of three scowling underdressed and over made-up women sashaying into the bar. On seeing they'd been noticed and recognised; the women broke into song to sing along with the tacky shit the DJ could only have been playing to wind people up. There were a lot of classic songs in the eighties, but it wasn't without it's mistakes.

'Three Bacardi's and Coke doll,' demanded the most forward of the three when reaching the bar. She very deliberately occupied the little space between Graeme and Laura; her smirking friends couldn't keep a secret. Cast adrift by Pauline and in a topsy-turvy little world of his own making, Graeme was apathetic to anything going on around him.

'Laura!' Spoken with a grimace poorly disguised as a smile, the woman at the bar tapped a fifty euro note up and down to the beat of the crappy song still playing. She had no class, and very little taste. Her two friends were blocking Liam's view of Graeme. There had been, or most likely still was some history between these people. No translator was required.

Regardless that they were women, Liam would still need the back-up of his best mate if there was going to be a fight. The last actual fight he'd been in was when he was in primary seven. There'd been tension between him and the school bully for some time, but he'd always managed to dodge a scrap by using his wit and intelligence. However, around two weeks before the schools were due to break up for the summer that year, and before everyone went off to their new secondary schools, Liam decided he'd had enough. In the school playground one day, during breaktime, he took a run and a lunge at his perpetual scourge. When sat on the chest of his fallen foe and pinning him to the ground, he'd screamed out his lungs with every punch he'd thrown at him. Thankfully, and as calculated, it was only a matter of seconds before the teacher who'd been monitoring the playground pulled him off his tormentor. Liam was suspended from school for his behaviour, and for the remainder of that term. The bully he'd beaten up, by now thinking Liam was a hard-case or mental, never bothered him again. And neither did anyone else. Liam's new-found reputation followed him all the way through secondary school and he never had one fight there either. Once you've been given a reputation, it stays with you. There are no exams on such things and no qualifications to be gained, but at a young age Liam had shown wit and intelligence of the highest order.

Liam's old gran though, well she hadn't heard these rumours. 'You're more of a worrier than a warrior,' she'd often tell him.

Intent on looking anywhere else other than the three women stood next to her, or Liam, Laura's eyes could have been blinking out a message in Morse-code.

Liam understood why diamonds were so popular, the way they caught the light to sparkle. But rubies? Why would a ruby stone be more popular and expensive than an emerald? Could it be something so basic as the colour red? Perhaps they embodied the blood that flows through our arteries and veins, all the way into our hearts. Maybe it was this that awakened a passion within. And another thing, does anyone know what smelling salts smell of? Are they an actual thing used in real life, or only as props in movies and on television? Whatever the answer to those questions, the stench hanging around his nostrils stirred Liam back to life. That, combined with-

'Alright mate?' It was a greeting of sorts from the ring leader of the three women at the bar. She spoke with a smile, but her eyes were scarred with disappointment and underachievement. Liam thought back to a time at work when two of his colleagues approached him at his desk. One of them was holding a polystyrene cup whilst using his other hand to cover the top of it. They'd asked Liam to breathe out, before then taking in a deep breath through his nostrils when the hand was removed. He was to guess the brand of aftershave hidden within. They'd both been in the staff toilets just before, to fart in the cup. That was the smell.

'You should watch yourself,' the woman at the bar went on. Only, she did so now with a more relatable frown and an unsubtle tip of her head. 'She's a bit of a slut. She has a reputation you know. And once you've been given a reputation, it stays with you.'

Liam's sudden discharge of, 'sorry', may have been misconstrued because the three women then took off with their drinks to waddle their way to a table. They went with a dance incorporating their elbows and their arses only. Realising he'd perhaps been daydreaming again, other than hearing Laura being called a slut, Liam had no idea what had just happened. Graeme was still debilitated, so no help at all. The acrid stench hanging around Liam's nostrils was then replaced by the scent of Laura's perfume. It lasted for a fleeting moment only, when she breezed past him to make her way out of club Tropicana. It was too late now, but why hadn't he mentioned how amazing she smelled? Idiot.

'What?'

The shove that woke Graeme from his comatose state achieved little more than allowing him to wipe away the drool from his mouth. Under normal circumstances he'd most likely have gotten away with it, but these retro disco lights were unforgiving. After a brief explanation as to what had just happened, as best as Liam could recall and paraphrase, Graeme's orders in reply were robust. 'Go and get her you plum. I'll stay here with Pauline, to let her know what's happened.'

After initially following the same route Laura had taken to leave, Liam decided instead to double-back deliberately (he walked backwards with intent), toward the table were the three women were now seated.

'Alright mate,' he began with a smile, and a glint in his eye. 'Let me guess,' he continued with a softly wagging finger. 'I'll just bet you're all feminists, right?' Three nodding though slightly apprehensive heads was his reply. The head-honcho woman, the one who'd made those comments at the bar (God love her), did also pipe up with an undaunted, 'of course we are.' Her words fought through a rasping chuckle that should have come with a health warning.

'Yeah. Equal pay and a seat in the boardroom, right?' With his fist clenched and raised in a show of solidarity, Liam smiled. As Graeme watched and wondered what was going on, and why wasn't Liam chasing after

Laura, he half-stood to debate with himself if he should go across and help. The way things were looking, he might have to step in to stop any potential carnage. Liam might draw back his clenched fist before going to town to land some hefty punches. Drinks would be thrown, glasses smashed, tables turned, hair pulled, and it would all end with Liam sitting on top of one of these women throwing punches down onto her chest. He'd have to rush over and pull him off her before the cops were called. Reminding himself that Liam hadn't had a single fight since that one way back in primary school, Graeme stayed put. 'Fuck sake,' he scoffed, before then scalding himself as he sat back down. 'Once you've been given a reputation.' With a shaking head, Graeme chuckled softly to sit himself comfortably and watch what his mate would actually do.

'What's the difference between a feminist and a capitalist with a fanny?' Liam asked the table of three whilst lowering slowly his still clenched fist. There was no reply. 'Ha!' Liam scoffed. The stench of peroxide and three for a tenner lipstick fighting a losing battle with either a cheap perfume, or more than likely a vaginal cream, suddenly hit him. But he had far more important issues to deal with. 'No, I don't know either. You're a bunch of stinking fucking hypocrites.' After punching his fist into the air, Liam left the building to go and look for Laura.

Still unsure what to do, if anything at all, Graeme was delighted to see Pauline returning from the bathroom. She'd been in there happily singing away to herself whilst having a pee. She'd also had to apply three different coats of lip gloss as she couldn't keep her lips from moving long enough to get it right first time. 'Don't tell me,' she smiled as she clicked from heel to toe, shuffling softly each step that drew her closer to Graeme again. 'Laura whispered something into Liam's ear, and now they're gone.'

So happy was he to see Pauline, and how happy she seemed to be, Graeme couldn't grasp what she'd asked. And certainly not what she was inferring. Gathering himself, he pointed to the table containing what he perceived to be the problem, 'those women.'

'Cows.' Pauline had eyes only for the table of three now, and Graeme was in no position to argue. And not at all envious.

Plucking the straw from her drink before throwing it onto the bar, Pauline lifted her glass. There was nothing but water and a melting ice-cube in there, but she'd committed so drained it anyway. 'Barbara,' Pauline cursed, as she began to fill Graeme in on some of the background. 'She was a failed teacher back home, and she's now a failing singer out here. All three of them are going through the change,' she snarled, as she slammed her empty glass down onto the bar. 'Changing from decent human-beings into absolute fucking cows.'

Impressed with Pauline's devotion to her friend and the energy she displayed in wanting to defend her, Graeme was about to ask what they should do. He hoped, wanted desperately to be able to show Pauline the same level of commitment that she herself was showing to Laura. 'Let's dance.' was perhaps the last thing Graeme expected to hear at this point, but that's what he got.

'But I can't- '

'Of course you can, you've just forgotten how.' As Pauline strode over to the little dancefloor, she half-turned to use her index finger to signal that this wasn't a request, it was an order. Graeme would have to improvise. Whilst making his way to join Pauline, he glanced over to where she was already looking. They both watched three women nervously negotiating ice-cubes to finish their drinks as quickly as possible. The greedy bitches didn't want to waste a drop.

'Hey Mickey. You know what to do,' Pauline shouted up to the DJ in his booth.

When he stepped onto the dancefloor timidly, Pauline gently eased Graeme to one side. She wanted a clearer view of anything that might get in her way. With a beaming smile the DJ removed an inner sleeve from its twelve-inch cover before then removing with care the twelve-inch vinyl disc itself. After spinning the outer edges of the disc around the palms of his hands he blew softly onto it. It was a kiss that only lovers of vinyl records would ever understand. Graeme didn't know this guy, but he liked him already.

Half expecting to hear a kitsch Toni Basil song, after hearing Pauline's shouted request, Graeme was delighted instead to hear the sound of an air attack warning booming from the speakers (the DJ had turned up the volume). Graeme recognised instantly the song being played.

Pauline finished rolling up her sleeves to conduct the orchestral piano section with a frightening elegance. In perfect time with the first crash of a symbol she pointed with resolve toward the table of the damned. A drum machine and the bass guitar agitated her feet into action. Yes, that bassline. By the time Holly had given his two words of instruction, Pauline was already on her way. She coasted across the floor from side-to-side as if floating on air. Was it atmospheric and aggressive? Probably. Was it a thing of beauty? Absolutely.

With his feet rooted to the floor Graeme's eyes danced with joy. With his head in the clouds playing keepie-uppie with the stars he double checked to see if there was any talcum powder on the dancefloor, to aid

Pauline's shuffling feet. There wasn't. The aroma was enchantment, by breathless. He felt twelve-foot-tall and the stars he played with were luminous decorations glued to the ceiling. Graeme couldn't dream of matching what Pauline was producing, but could anyone? Carefree and nonchalant she didn't care who was watching, or if no-one was. She had no urge, want or need to be seen, to be liked or to be popular. And yet she could never have been wanted so much.

On looking up to see Graeme standing still and studying her every move, Pauline gazed into his eyes. She lit up a firework smile when singing to him the lyrics of the song, 'tell the world that you're winning. Loving life, loving life.' She then stopped for a moment, and when leaning in toward him she pinched gently one of Graeme's cheeks as an unspoken thank-you. It couldn't possibly have been that innocent little squeeze that sent him dizzy, but when Graeme found himself spinning around in a cumbersome pirouette, it did reveal three empty glasses sitting at an otherwise empty table.

When finding his balance again, if not his poise, Graeme raised his hands in front of him when he thought Pauline's were reaching out for them. Pauline's hands weren't looking for anything. They swished back and forth in front of her as a counter balance to her shuffling feet, swinging hips and shifting shoulders. Compelled for a moment to try and move his feet in relative harmony too, because love can make a fool of anyone, Graeme was delighted when Pauline recognised his awkwardness. She did then take hold of his hands into her own, and when leaning forward again she stood on her tip-toes to whisper into his ear.

After initially stepping back nervously, Pauline was at once euphoric when she understood the look on

Graeme's face. It wasn't something she'd ever witnessed before herself, but there was no mistaking it. Squeezing his hands in her own she led him off the dancefloor. He was still struck dumb, but Graeme's smile widened even more when Pauline thrust up the middle finger of her free hand behind her. 'Hey Mickey,' she shouted. 'You're still a prick. But cheers anyway.'

As Pauline and Graeme were leaving Tropicana, behind them Mickey had already put on his next record of choice. To the beat of the original Frankie classic, with a grin and his thrusting hips, he was dry-humping an architectural pillar when he shouted back, 'relax Pauline, relax.'

13

Red sky at night and red sky in the morning. Such was his frustration Liam couldn't remember the next lines to those verses. The smouldering cloak overhead was more than dramatic and all-encompassing, but at this juncture there was only one option open to him. He had to walk the length of this seemingly endless promenade with no distinct end in sight, because in the distance stood Laura. Separated and rising above the disordered and objectionable herd that prevaricated with abandon around her, her eyes swelled with magic and shone like beacons to guide him. And the downhill slope of his path was sure to make his journey easier, rather than being a foreboding metaphor. Laura's blonde hair and white robe-like dress rippled impertinently behind. The wind was with Liam.

A glance over his right shoulder showed an almost deserted beach, until running out from the wild blue sea came the two friends who'd deserted him prior to coming on holiday. Proud in their swim trunks, Mark and Gareth offered up their artificial pleasantries and phoney smiles. After glancing in front to make sure Laura was still waiting, when he turned again to question his friends, they taunted him with rude gestures. They'd been joined now by a gaggle of bikini clad beauties, and they too mocked. Whilst dancing provocatively they opened bottles of champagne with their pursed lips to douse themselves in bubbles.

In no mood for a debate, let alone a scrap Liam turned his other cheek instead, to look across to his left-hand side.

Beneath the rows of American styled bleacher seating, scurrying rats quarrelled with slithering snakes for clear space in the dirt. Above them all sat Mr McCullogh, one of the men who'd been entrusted with providing an education for Liam in primary school. He shook his head at the contents of the manuscript he was reading, before washing down his contempt with a swig of whisky. In a puff of electric blue smoke Mr McCullogh fell through the gaps in the seating to run indiscriminately with the critters below. Taking his bottle of whisky with him, he left the manuscript behind. Discarded. All along the rows of seating were others from Liam's past and present. They were a motley crew, all of them. Whilst some had two faces, most of them were users and abusers, fakes, frauds and phoneys. After losing eye contact with them, they too seemed apathetic to what they read.

On tearing his eyes from the bleachers to face front once more, Liam felt the cold steel of a huge iron gate pressing against his nose. A sturdy padlock and chain upon it blocked his way. Beyond the gate and through the gaps in the bars he watched Laura turn to walk away. With the wind catching against her dress to hasten her departure she was out of sight within seconds. The wind had picked up, and it was against Liam.

When turning to make a desperate plea for help, Liam found only the people who mocked him. Mark and Gareth on the one side joined in with some of his own family, old friends and acquaintances on the other. Together they pointed and sniggered. When he looked down to see why they laughed so hard, he saw what they could see. Wearing no clothes, he was stark-raving bollock naked. With his knees buckling underneath and his head in a spin, Liam let himself go. Falling – falling - falling-.

'Alright mate. Nightmare?'

'What? Oh right, yeah. But we'll be going home soon. So-'

The bedroom door banging against one of the beds when opened caused Liam to jump upright with a start. No matter how cool he tried to play it, it was obvious to Graeme his mate had fallen asleep on top of his made bed. Fully clothed, and alone.

'I meant the dream you were having. Anyway, I take it you didn't catch up with her. Laura, I mean. Last-night. I did knock three times. You know, just in case. Are you okay?'

'I'm fine mate. But I didn't see Laura, after she'd left Tropicana. Have you seen her?' A cursory glance up caused Liam to retie his left shoe twice. 'Was she home, at Pauline's? Is she okay?'

'Yeah mate, she's good. She didn't come home though. She sent Pauline a text saying she wanted some time to herself, and that she wouldn't be going in to work today.'

'That's something, at least. So, what's happening now?' Liam gave a hesitant chuckle. He knew the answer to the question he was about to ask, but it had to be done. 'Have you been drafted in to lend a hand in the café?'

'Nah mate. I can't boil an egg, you know that.' Graeme returned the chuckle in kind. 'The cafés staying closed today. Me and Pauline are going to – well, just spend the day together.'

'Chuffed for you mate, and I hate to put a dampener on things. But remember we're leaving tonight!'

'I know. The coach leaves for the airport at eight-thirty, that's why I'm here. I'm going to pack my case and then jump in the shower, before I go back to Pauline's for-'

Pulling his suitcase out from underneath his bed hid any change of colour to Graeme's face, and a faintly whistled tune signalled he was saying no more. The smile on Liam's face contradicted the forceful blows he handed out to his pillows as he tried to rearrange them for some comfort. Suitcase packed and a change of clothes readied, Graeme extended his hand and a smile before dancing into the tiny en-suite. When laying back down Liam listened to the joy in the voice from behind the shower curtain. Most of the songs being belted out professed in their lyrics the wonders of being in love. Not even two battered and lifeless pillows could diminish Liam's delight for his best friend's current state of glee.

'What have you got planned for today?' Other than he'd thrown his legs up and onto his bed, Graeme noticed that Liam hadn't budged an inch.

Liam refrained from asking Graeme why he sang in the shower but whistled outside of it. He couldn't be sure it was even possible to maintain a whistle under a shower. He'd give it a try himself, later.

'I'm not sure. I'll probably sit on the beach for a bit, see if I can pick up a little bit of colour.' It was only after he'd raised his fingers to highlight the lack of a tan on his arms that led Liam to realise, he'd been using his thumbs to tap out a beat onto his tummy. Graeme's expansive tribute to the music of nineteen-eighty-something seemed to be complete, and Liam's feet eventually got the memo too. With his ankles crossed the toes of one of his training shoes had been tapping against the other.

'Have you looked outside mate? It's typical last day of holiday weather. Cloudy as hell.'

Looking to his left-hand side but annoyingly unable to see around corners, Liam could only shrug his shoulders. He mumbled something about going to the bar, or to the shops – or - something.

'Didn't you see the sky this morning?' Graeme asked. 'It was amazing. But you know what they say, shepherds warning.'

With Graeme having a reputation for not being a morning person, whether it was carried out through a sense of duty, social-conditioning or just without prior thought, Liam fell into the lads together on holiday trap to question him on his probable lack of sleep. And therefore his manliness. 'Sorry mate. You don't have to answer any of that, I'm just tired. I'll maybe stay here and grab forty-winks, before the bus comes.'

'It's fine mate.' Graeme reassured, before sitting down and onto the edge of his bed. He told Liam how he and Pauline had indeed had very little sleep. He told how they'd danced whilst listening to her extensive record collection, most of which he knew and some of which he also owned. They'd also talked, a lot. Fulfilment did eventually weigh heavy on his head when he lowered it to intimate that yes, they had indeed enjoyed each other's company.

When Graeme's head rose sharply again to exhibit a frivolous grin, and it was complimented with a blurted out opening statement of, 'I know you're going to think I'm fucking mental mate.' Liam had no idea what was going to follow. 'I've not even said anything to Pauline,' Graeme went on with haste. 'I mean, how could I? Like I say, it's fucking mental.'

Uncrossing his legs to sit up on his bed, in unison with Graeme's sudden leap up from his, Liam didn't have to wait too long for Graeme's full confession.

'I could stay here mate. Not get on that plane. I mean, what's stopping me?'

Whilst a gentle nodding of the head can be read in different ways by different people in different situations, without saying a single word, Liam's flattened lips were ultimately the giveaway. He'd have preferred more time to think, so's not to hurt his mates feelings or be a negative influence on his desires. What he didn't want to do, and wouldn't under any circumstances, was go for the easy option to say the two words beginning with the letters H and R. And he wasn't thinking about those bastards back home in Human Resources.

'It's okay. I know it's stupid mate, you can tell me. It's just that.' A three-sixty spin that began with clenched fists ended with Graeme's fingers outstretched. It also brought a smile and a jolt of renewed confidence to convince Liam how serious he was. 'I can't explain it mate. I wish I could, but I can't.'

A considered look around their magnolia covered room devoid of any character (other than that one framed picture of two kids wearing ponchos), brought relaxed lips. Liam's nodding head now took on new meaning, and he found the words to back it up, 'I get it,' he began. 'She's all you can think about, every minute of every day. When you're with her you want to talk non-stop, but you have to hold yourself back because you're frightened to say the wrong thing. And yet, the truth is. The truth is, there are no words. There's nothing you could say that would adequately illustrate how you truly feel about her. She's the last thing you think about at night and the first thing you think of in the morning. And in between she haunts your dreams.'

With Liam's focus evidently taken by the tacky car boot sale picture hanging on the wall, Graeme mirrored briefly his friends' circumspect disposition. He then turned to grab hold of and open the room door. 'Cheers mate,' he shouted, before pausing to observe that he once again had eye contact with Liam. 'I just want to say.' Stopping himself suddenly, to look along the long and empty lobby of the hotel for the appropriate words, Graeme found instead his true feelings. 'I know this holiday was going to be a kind of goodbye. I know we're all going to be taking different roads, and I'm cool with that - The other's I mean. You though. I'm going to miss you mate. I hope we can stay in touch, the two of us.'

No interpreter was required to translate Liam's nodding head this time, even when it was followed by a descending hand and a jovial instruction to 'fuck-off'.

The door swinging open again before it had even had time to close over, revealed Graeme's beaming face again. 'All of that stuff you just said, you should write it down mate. You could put it in one of those self-help brochure things. Somebody would probably pay you good money for stuff like that.'

'Fuck-off.' Liam was down to just one pillow when his other hastened the closing of the bedroom door and the departure of his mate. In need of a stretch, a stroll onto the balcony to see what the weather was doing would kill two birds with one stone. Sure enough it was cloudy overhead, but it didn't look like it was going to rain any time soon. And certainly not on Graeme's day. He may not have been kicking his heels as he went, but he was waving to random strangers as he skipped merrily on his way to see Pauline again.

Returning to the solitude of his own company, Liam stole the four pillows from the other beds before throwing himself back down onto his own. Flat-out and considering what to do next, he exhaled a modest grunt. 'Self-fucking help,' he despaired. 'My arse,' he continued, before burying his head under his stack of freshly plundered pillows from the beds his mates weren't using.

14

Showered and shaved, although perhaps the after-shave had been unnecessary, Liam had been walking for around an hour. Unsure at first whether he was hungry he'd decided it was a good fried breakfast he wanted. Unfortunately he didn't know where to find a good place, at least not one that was open. Popping his head into some of the bars and clubs was no use either. If he'd been back home, he'd have no problem in finding a lonely old drunk who would be glued to a barstool, one he could spill his guts to. But he wasn't in England anymore.

Finding himself stood outside one of the bars he'd previously frequented, Liam read again the bawdy advertising board and wondered if they ever bothered updating it. Written on there, amongst a few other acts, appearing tonight at nine o'clock would be the comedy of 'Laura Laughs'. There was a good six hours or so before any of the entertainment was due to start and no-one behind the bar, let alone any sympathetic ears, but Liam had nothing else to do.

'What can I get you?'

After gingerly making his way toward a little stage when seeing no-one in the pub, Liam turned to see where the voice was coming from. Instinctively making his way to the bar, when he reached it and then looked over the top of the old wooden counter, he saw a man in a wheelchair. He was busily restocking a fridge.

'What can I get you mate?' the man asked again. When he turned around in his chair, he was clearly annoyed at having to ask the same question twice. Either that or he was just a miserable old sod.

Not sure what he did want, Liam didn't have a response to the question put to him. Freezing under the glare of the now sinister looking barman, after a little umming and ahhing, he managed a soft apology of sorts and an instruction that he didn't want a drink.

'Well, you're in the wrong fucking place.'

Charming.

'I was looking for – Well wondering, if Laura was around.' Pressured into talking by the barman's piercing eyes, Liam couldn't help himself. 'Laura laughs. The stand-up comic. Sorry, that's probably not her surname. I don't know what her surname is. She's playing here tonight, at nine. It says so, on the board outside. I saw her before. In here I mean.' Managing to shut himself up before spewing out anymore of his random thoughts and rambling nonsense, Liam wanted to bash his head onto the counter. The barman didn't like him before he'd opened his mouth, what must he be thinking now?

'Is your name Liam?'

'Yeah.' His head hadn't made it onto the counter, but it might as well have. Recoiling when asked that question Liam tried to steady his ship, 'how do you know that?' he continued, when his head found its bearings again.

'I'm a mind reader,' the barman laughed, before realising he'd left himself open to more questions and he was far too busy for that. 'I'll tell your fortune for twenty-quid, if you want.' If this guy didn't have any spare money to buy a drink, it stood to reason he wouldn't want to shell out any of his hard-earned on a side-show palm reading. Tight-arsed sod. As soon as he pissed off, there'd be peace and quiet to get his fridges done. Wait until he gets his hands on that lazy little Spaniard, for not doing as he should.

'How would your mind reading skills enable you to tell my fortune? They're two different – Well, talents - For the lack of a better word. Surely?'

'Alright smart-arse.' Caught in the act, the barman turned again to fill his fridges. 'She's not around. Come back at nine, and you can buy a drink then.'

The squeak of a toilet door being cautiously opened was also the cue for the barman to push himself up and out of his chair. When looking over the bar counter and out onto the street, he saw the same thing Laura could. Peeking out from behind the small opening she'd created, they watched Liam walking away.

'He seems like a nice fella,' said Yoz. He watched with interest as Laura made her way almost ballerina like toward the window. 'In a vulnerable sort of way. The poor sap,' he continued with a chuckle. Returning to the bar, Laura slumped herself down onto it with a groan. Yoz's deliberately contradictory review of Liam had brought him no further information. Laura had been checking the weather when she'd seen Liam approach. With his hands lodged in his pockets and his head bowed forlornly, he'd been kicking out at the innocent stones in his path. He hadn't seen Laura dash inside for cover.

'Can I offer you some advice?'

Laura's lips audibly reverberated against the bar top, and what she said wasn't clear.

'I don't want to get involved, but- '

'Fuck-off Yoz.' Sensing a puddle of her own saliva beginning to form around her cursing mouth, Laura stood upright to wipe the bar with her sweater. Her vulgar frown wasn't the result of her damp sleeve though, it was the thought of anybody else's saliva that could have been there before hers. Some of the punters that came in here didn't need to lay there head down to drool, they managed to do it standing up.

'I'm just saying – look. I know and understand, sort of, why you don't want to get too involved with anyone. Seriously I mean. As in – Long-term-'

'Not in the mood Yoz.'

Pushing himself up and out from his chair again to watch Laura walk to the front door, Yoz without saying anything assumed she too would be leaving. Wondering briefly why kids so hated to listen to advice from their elders, his mind was then taken instead with the size of his biceps. Lately, it seemed he'd had reason to do far more push-ups than most professional athletes.

'Can I stay here again tonight?'

'What? Yeah, course you can.' Surprised by Laura's return, Yoz smiled as he stretched out his arms to show-off his muscle-bound though perhaps slightly cramped arms.

'Cheers. Just for tonight.' When resting her elbows onto the bar Laura thought about, but then resisted the temptation to lay down her weary head. Not even in the spot she now wiped clean for a second time.

'Let me say one thing,' Yoz pleaded. After several dismissive uhu uhu's, Laura agreed to hear him out. She had a request of her own anyway, so this could be a bargaining chip for her. All things aside, it would be her rent payment for the night. Taxed, always taxed. Isn't life a bitch. 'Only if you promise me something in return first,' she demanded. With more than a hint of suspicion and a little deliberation, because she was a canny one, Yoz agreed to Laura's demand and hoped he wouldn't live to regret it. He was forever pleading poverty so couldn't suddenly manufacture wads of cash, if that's what she was after.

'No offence.' As soon as she'd uttered those first two words, the look facing her from behind the bar had changed from a guarded suspicion to concerned anxiety. Laura wondered what he'd been expecting her to say or ask. Surely, he could have guessed what was coming next. 'Last night was fucking atrocious.' As soon as the penny dropped (because Yoz never missed an opportunity to pick one up), Laura was confronted by a raised and proud smooth chin, an inflated chest and the face of a zealous teenager. She knew loads of spotty teenagers, but the grinning face behind the bar belonged to Yoz. 'It sounded like a fucking zoo in here last night. I'm not kidding. The both of you. If she's staying over again tonight, try and keep it down a bit.'

'That's what.' Stopping to wipe away the drizzle of snot that managed to liberate itself from his nose, and through his raucous laughter, Yoz tried in vain to continue. 'That's exactly what I wanted to talk to you about-'

'Eeeew.'

'No, fuck-off. Not what I was doing. What we were doing, well not exactly.'

'Eeeew.' There weren't any other appropriate words to fit the situation, or to accurately describe Laura's current displeasure. Where was Pauline when she was needed?

'Look. I'm stuck in this fucking contraption.' After banging his hands against the wheels of his chair to highlight his predicament, Yoz then went on again, only in a more solemn tone now. 'I never thought I'd find anyone else. Not after your – look. All I'm trying to say is – you never know. Don't slam all of the doors closed - just because.'

With no comeback from Laura, which was a rarity, and a moment of reflection, Yoz stopped there. He'd said all he needed to for the time-being. It was up to her. He'd offer his support in whatever she chose to do, he always did.

A stroll to the front door and another look outside brought no surprises for Laura. When returning, she tapped her hand twice gently onto the bar to get Yoz's attention, before letting him know she was going for a lie-down.

'Hey, Laura.'

On turning around to see what Yoz wanted, Laura watched him let out an animalistic lion like roar. 'A fucking zoo,' he then muttered. Laura left with a grimace that again implied, 'eeeew'. 'I'm the King of the world,' she heard being shouted. She didn't turn around to see the proud man in his wheelchair with his arms raised aloft to an otherwise empty bar. Yoz couldn't be bothered with filling his fridges now, there was more to life.

Sitting on high on top of a volcanic rock Liam had the world at his feet, at least he should have. If he were to look across to his left and then to his right, there were other islands grouped with this one. They were all of them overflowing with venues selling fun and laughter, song and dance, and perhaps some other even more exotic excesses. Alone with his thoughts as the swirling wind caught hold to cause a little dust storm, Liam examined his life past and what was still to come. The lizard on an adjoining rock who'd kept him company for the past few minutes didn't have any such worries. Then again, perhaps it did. Why else would it have scampered off to leave him alone again? High enough to reach up and grab at the clouds suppressing the sun, Liam wondered if the neighbouring islands were not to his left and right after-all, but instead in front and behind him. Other than being on Tenerife, Liam had no idea where in the world he was.

Whenever music is discussed within groups of a certain generation, a common question sometimes asked would be, 'what was the first single you ever bought?' In Liam's case he could answer with pride that his was a song called 'Clint Eastwood' by 'Gorillaz'. His answer would usually be met with agreeable nods of accepting heads regarding his taste in music. It was CD singles he'd bought that day, but it could have been worse. Just a few months after those first purchases, a little silver box came over from America that allowed people to lease their favourite songs by download, rather than owning them outright. However, he wouldn't ever confess to buying two CD singles that day. The other one was by a band called 'Hearsay'. Why was it so difficult to be open and honest in life, to freely express your opinions and emotions?

Pure and simple. Unfortunately, life is anything but.

Unbegrudging, but trying not to think too much about his mate Graeme and what he'd be getting up to right now, Liam emptied his mind of any and all thoughts to take in the scenery. Jealousy can be a love and a hate at the same time. It can also consume and eat away at one's soul.

Walking into the hallway of the little Spanish apartment, on the left-hand side was a shower room. Its window was open to disperse lingering steam. The shower curtain was wet and there was a used towel in the sink. The toilet seat was raised. Across from the bathroom was a small well-kept and clean though sparse bedroom. Other than a few posters on the wall and an acoustic guitar leaning lazily against a wall for decoration, there was little else inside to offer any clues as to who the absentee occupant might be. The bed hadn't been slept in. Further on up the hall was a small kitchen kept so clean and tidy it could only belong to a person, or persons who ate out often. Or worked in the catering industry. Facing the kitchen was another bedroom. Sheets from an unmade bed had been strewn with abandon across the floor. On top of a little dressing table sat a pile of books, and on top of those books was a box containing the board game Scrabble. Opening the sitting-room door increased the volume of the music being played. It also revealed Pauline and Graeme. Sat together on the floor and facing one-another in front of a little record-player turntable, in between and connecting them was a substantial pile of already played vinyl records.

With the cold-blooded critters abandoning him too, Liam tried to pick himself up and off a meagre rock to spend this last afternoon on holiday alone. With around three hours to burn before the bus would take him to the airport, he didn't want to be tempted into having a drink. On the rare occasions he did have a 'blow out', Liam was a happy drunk, before then morphing into the sleepy drunk. In no rush, and with no firm plan of action he decided to avoid the main strip. His descent down the steep gradient that seemed to take as long as his ascent confused Liam. He had to remind himself that he'd stopped periodically, to look around at his surroundings. A view of one of the beaches showed it to be forsaken and its sea was agitated and cold. The sky above was still full and moody and yet to fully commit in what direction it would be heading. Liam could empathise.

With his hands in his pockets and in a world of his own making, Liam half jumped when hearing a woman call out his name. When Pauline let go of Graeme's hand to run toward him, the lack of any direct sunlight could not diminish the ray of sunshine bursting from her gold dress with its shimmering tassels, or her broadening smile. 'Hiya,' she shouted, with an element of curiosity. Although she wasn't half as puzzled as Graeme was when he'd felt his hand go suddenly cold. 'You look lost,' she continued, when reaching Liam's side to stroke his arm.

Smiling to return the welcome before giving a nod to his oncoming though slightly lagging best mate, Liam misread Pauline's remark, 'yeah well, you know. It's only been a short break, so I haven't had time to get to know the place.'

'Silly.' Pauline laughed, before urging Graeme to catch-up. After reaching her hand through Liam's arm she repeated the trick with Graeme. 'That's not what I mean. Come on.'

With a man attached at either side, Pauline had them both glancing over and past her. They wondered if she'd perhaps gone a little cuckoo. She'd begun by telling a tale of little boys in the school playground who would take a fancy to a little girl. The boy would tease her and maybe even pull her hair. She spoke of how, as adults we now recognise this as the shy little boys' way of trying to have some form of contact with the girl. Any contact, no matter how warped it may be. She then seemed to digress absolutely and in an instant, when talking in detail about tides turning. Neither Liam or Graeme had a chance to give any of these topics much thought, as she seemed to be meandering between many different subjects in quick succession. Whilst Liam put it down to a lustful hangover,

Graeme remembered a time when his big brother was so excited to have brought home a new vinyl single from the record shop. He'd shouted Graeme, who was still a child at the time to come through to his bedroom and listen to it with him. That song was 'Common People' by 'Pulp'. By the time the song had ended, only to be played again straight after, Graeme knew it was a little bit different and beautifully mystifying. Even as a young boy of five years old, he remembered It as being something magical he would never tire of listening to. Graeme had never felt anything like that before, or since. Until today and now, with Pauline by his side.

'Here we are.'

Unbeknown to Liam and Graeme, as they'd been blindly agreeing with Pauline's eloquent though slightly unbalanced monologue, they'd all taken a back-road short-cut to, and were now standing directly outside of Yosser's bar. Whilst Pauline marched on in shouting for Yoz with an elongated and demanding vowel, Liam and Graeme stared blankly at one-another. Until Pauline ordered them both to get a shift on and join her.

Recognising instantly the voice bellowing out his name, Yoz hoisted himself up once more. This time it was to welcome his number two girl. 'Look at you,' he hollered. 'All dressed up in your elegant gold dress. You look amazing, what's the occasion? And more importantly, am I invited?'

'Never mind me. Look at you, fancy pants.' Pauline blushed and beamed as one when leaning across the bar. 'A new shirt, a designer one. And clean shaven.'

Yoz's changing facial expressions alerted Pauline that she'd been joined by her companions. Knowing their places, it was one at either side again.

'This is Liam,' announced Pauline, when using her hands to illustrate which of the two she meant.

'Yeah, I know. We've met, briefly. He was in here a couple of hours ago.'

Pauline's initial surprise at Yoz's revelation was then amplified tenfold after Liam's response. 'Yeah,' he grinned. 'But let's be honest. You knew I'd be coming back, didn't you?' Raising his hands up to the side of his head and by his ears with his fingers splayed, Liam was making what could only be described as a ghostly wailing sound. With no idea what he was playing at, and slightly concerned for his safety, Pauline looked behind the bar for Yoz's reaction. He'd always deny it (whether he didn't want to be a hero, or just didn't want anyone to know he'd touched another man down there), but Pauline was sure she'd once seen Yoz punch a man in the balls. Some guy had been bothering the regulars in the bar, women mostly, and was generally being a bit of a twat. Anyway, Yoz claims he never touched the bloke and that his legs must have given out on account of all the cheap booze he'd been drinking. And not even in his pub, he'd always go on to emphasise.

Appreciating Liam's good-humoured reference to him saying earlier that he was a fortune teller, 'well played sir.' was Yoz's eccentric response. He bowed forward in his chair as he spoke. Pauline had no idea what was going on, but at least needn't worry about anyone else being punched in the balls. When taking a turn and a step to her right, she then radiated, 'and this is Graeme.' Having Pauline wrapped tight around his upper body meant Graeme could move only one of his arms, and even then, only just. He did raise it, along with a nervous smile to say hello.

'Now the dress makes sense. You look fantastic.' To put two and two together was a dawdle for Yoz.

'What about you? And - are you wearing the aftershave we got for you, last Christmas?'

'I am indeed.' When raising his chin to expose his neck and his joy, Yoz almost blushed. 'For the first time today. And very nice it is too. Thank-you.'

'Hold on a minute.' Pauline's slanted head and constricting eyes were perhaps an indication she was onto something, but they were by no means a forewarning of what was to follow. 'Have you — are you?'

Before he'd had a chance to look away to suppress his guilty smile, it was already too late. Knowing she was onto something, Pauline leapt up and onto the bar counter to lay belly down on top of it. 'Tell me you miserable old bugger,' she demanded. 'You've gone and found yourself a woman, haven't you?' The frantic kicking of her legs and the wagging of a finger was beginning to take Pauline's breath away. She pleaded for confirmation. 'Come on Yoz. Is she in here now? Whisper it to me.'

With little to no idea what was going on, or any clue what he'd now signed up for, Graeme stood flabbergasted. Liam had other things to occupy him and he'd been busily scouring every corner of the bar. Although he couldn't see anything of interest to him directly, he did think it prudent to inform Pauline about the dirty old man perving on her. Stood by his table whilst ignoring the slapping hands of his wife, Bill was using his own to mimic a pair of binoculars. His hands thrusting back and forth suggested he might have zoom lenses.

'Please Pauline.' It was Yoz's turn to slant his head. 'Tell me you're wearing underwear?'

With a smile and a cool as you like not a care in the world attitude, Pauline rolled onto her side to plant an elbow down onto the bar. When resting her chin into the palm of her open hand she very calmly said, 'it's getting draughty up here.'

Rescued from the bar with the aid of Liam and Graeme, no sooner had Pauline's feet hit the floor and she was turning around to give Bill a wave. After raising her hands in the air, in a 'yeah look at me' fashion, she then gave him a twirl. When then bending at her knees she blew over two kisses, one of them was for Bill and the other for Christina. As Bill sat himself down to give his wife a cuddle, Yoz could sense the two lads obvious disorientation. 'It's alright,' he began. 'He worked for the BBC in the sixties and the seventies. He's probably seen a lot worse.'

With her mouth astounded and her jaw to the floor, Pauline turned accusingly.

'Worse was probably a bad choice of word.' Thinking he'd embarrassed Pauline in front of her new beau, Yoz's apology came quickly. 'The wrong word. Help me out, you're far better with the words than me.'

Unable to speak because of her squeezing lips, Pauline turned to Graeme for his input. Other than a shrug and a simper, 'I've got nothing,' was all he could offer.

'And he's been on Countdown,' snarled Pauline.

'Fuck-off!' Crimewatch was the only television show the kind of people Yoz usually mixed with had been on.

'He has,' laughed Pauline. 'I promise. And he's a two-time champion.' Her smile outshone her dress.

'Fuck-off!' In no uncertain terms, Yoz testified he wasn't lying about his somewhat limited vocabulary. He'd watched Countdown umpteen times, mostly with Pauline, but he'd always struggle to score anything higher than a four on the letters games. The numbers game though, that was more to his liking.

'He's got two teapots, and he's going to show me them,' Pauline continued. 'He says I can hold them both in my hands, if I want to.'

'No. I can't.' Between his howls, Yoz made a mental note to start carrying a handkerchief for his runny nose. 'Christ sake Pauline, you can't just line them up for me like that. Honestly. You know I love you as one of my own, but sometimes you make it too easy sweetheart.' When looking to the lads for support, Yoz got nothing from Graeme. He still looked a little shell-shocked and unsure what planet he was on. Liam on the other hand returned the earlier compliment. 'Well played sir,' he said, whilst placing one hand on his belly to bow forward.

Still unsure what was going on between those two, Pauline shook her head to quiz Yoz again on his dapper look and any potential love interest. Like a magic wand, a bending of Yoz's finger that urged her to come in closer made Pauline's hair stand on end. From this alone she understood the lady in question must be present. Before moving in to be told who the lady was, Pauline couldn't help but glance around for one last guess as to who it might be. Graeme and Liam followed suit. There was no outstanding candidate, which only made Pauline tingle even more. Barely able to contain herself, she edged in for the big reveal.

'There's these three women- '

Was as far as Yoz managed to get before Pauline jumped back to squeal in a frenzy. After calming herself down, only just, she whispered through the hands she held tight against her mouth, 'not the merry widows.'

The bending finger that had been used to summon Pauline forward was now pressed tight against Yoz's strangled lips. Through a sense of urgency it was joined in its job of work by the corresponding finger of his other hand. 'Shh,' he smiled. 'Yeah. Although, they're not widows. Well one of them is, and the other two are divorcees. They've been coming here for a few years now. It was a getaway for the divorcees to help their friend get over her loss. Well now. One of the divorcees, Jane's her name, well we got talking and she told me she's liked me since the first time she saw me. Who'd have thought it eh? And all this time she's been keeping it to herself, until last night. Listen though, it's top secret. Her friends don't know, and I'm not sure if she wants them to know. Yet.'

'Which one's Jane?' Pauline asked in a hushed tone, when removing her hands from her mouth to rest them on her chest. A sedate and apologetic shaking of the head was the only reply she got. Half of Pauline couldn't turn around for fear of letting on to Jane, whichever one she was, that the cat had been let out the bag. And the other half was compelled to look a while longer at the overflowing ecstasy behind the bar.

'Imagine keeping something like that to yourself for all that time.' Pauline spoke without thinking, but from his grandstand seat it struck a chord with Liam.

'To hell with it,' said Pauline, as she tried to pull herself together again. With a considerate head and a serious face she turned to look at the gathered clientele. After slowly spinning around and then to a stop, she was immediately confronted with the merry widows staring back at her (one widow and two divorcees). They'd all three of them noted various commotions and disturbances at the bar. If Pauline didn't have their full and undivided attention already, her next squeal certainly sealed the deal. Unable to contain herself any longer, she bent at the knees again. This time she also offered a hearty double thumbs up accompanied with a wink. Whilst two of the ladies returned their own subdued and confused waves back, the other (on the blind-side of her friends) settled her hands down onto the high back of her chair. After resting her chin down onto her hands she sent back a vibrant smile that said thank-you. There was no doubting now which of the three was Jane, and she was lovely.

'I'm so happy for you. You deserve it.' When she turned to face Yoz again, Pauline clasped her hands together to place them onto her chest. Underneath those, her galloping heart raced.

'Thank-you. And likewise, I assume? Now. Enough of that mushy stuff. What are you having to drink?'

Faced on both sides with protesting fingers, after apologising to Yoz for not being able to hang around for a drink, Pauline reminded Graeme (with her eyes mostly) that they were supposed to be going back to hers for 'something to eat'. Taking the unsubtle hint immediately Graeme lowered his hand with a grin. Liam also fell into line, although he did bemoan in jest that no-one was offering him anything to eat.

'This one could eat for two anyway,' Pauline laughed when hugging Graeme. 'Bloody ravenous he is.'

When explaining they'd only come in to see if Laura was around, Pauline hesitantly questioned if she was here. She questioned some more when Yoz was inconsistent and non-committal in his replies. Knowing Yoz would never lie to her outright, without good reason, Pauline decided not to push him any further. He'd already stated the obvious, that Laura would be onstage at nine o'clock. 'Read the bloody chalkboard,' he grumbled. When turning to tend to his already fully stocked fridges he decried the money he'd wasted on his advertising campaign, 'eight bloody euro's I paid for that blackboard.' Humming and hawing as he delicately swapped one bottle of lager with another, he then went on. 'You can look at it on your way out. Seeing as how you're not buying any drinks.' With Yoz intent on not divulging anything he thought best not to, Pauline told him to chill-out, and that they were leaving.

'It was a pleasure meeting you.' No sooner had Pauline conceded defeat, and Yoz had spun himself around to offer a handshake to Graeme. 'You take good care of her now, you hear me?'

'Yeah, or vice-versa.' Graeme half whimpered as Yoz's grip tightened on his own.

'And you best listen to him,' Pauline demanded of Graeme through a grin and a pointing finger. 'I once saw him punch a man in the balls.'

'He was asking for it.' Yoz finally confessed, before then releasing his handshake with Graeme to edge down to Liam. 'You too mate, take care. And I'll see you all again, hopefully.'

Making their way to the exit, it wasn't long before Pauline and the lads heard a familiar voice give off a sudden shout, 'you'll have me in the bankruptcy courts.' When Liam and Graeme looked behind, they saw two wildly oscillating arms flashing back and forth behind the bar. They also saw most of the customers laughing to see such hilarity. Pauline was nonplussed and walked on, she'd seen and heard it all before.

'Are you coming back to mine? For, you know. A quick bite. Before you have to leave.' Lowering her head to give Graeme the freedom to decline her offer with no pressure, Pauline's hips took on a mind of their own. As they swayed back and forth gently from left to right, she waited for a reply.

Pauline made one of the best fried breakfasts he'd ever had, but Graeme wasn't hungry. And when looking across to Liam he could feel a sense of loss. However, the quandary was; this wasn't just an offer of breakfast, this was five-star a-la-carte fine dining.

'Yeah,' laughed Liam, when he took the decision out of Graeme's hands. 'He's going with you. We've a bit of time left and I'm going for a little walk, to clear my head. Go and enjoy yourselves.' A heartfelt thank-you with a sloppy peck on his cheek, accompanied with an audible 'mwah', was Liam's reward for being such a good friend to them both. Pauline then darted off to leave the two of them alone for a bit.

'Go on mate. And regarding what you said to me in the room this morning, boy do I get it. She's a cracker. Whatever you choose to do, you have my support. In fact, don't mess it up.'

'Cheers.' Trying to control his hands as they danced back and forth at his side, Graeme gathered himself to continue. 'Another thing I said. I know, and I understand you might be moving on with your life. Other things, places perhaps. And other people too. I get all of that. But I think I said earlier that I hope we stay in touch. Scratch that. Promise me - promise me you'll always stay in touch.'

'Come on. You two can kiss and make-up at the airport.' She didn't particularly want to break up the bromance playing out in front of her, but as Pauline stood by the open door of her waiting taxi, she knew better than most that these foreign drivers took liberties with the fares they charged. Especially when they hear an English accent, and the meter was already running. Welcoming the chance to break what was becoming an emotional silence, when they turned as one Liam and Graeme watched Pauline throw her arms in the air to perform another three-sixty turn. The sun had made up its mind to break free from the clouds and light up her golden tassels.

'Aren't you hungry?' she giggled, before jumping into the back of the cab. Once sat down she shouted out an apology from the still open door when remembering she'd gone commando today. She'd felt another draught.

'A vision of love wearing boxing gloves.' Graeme almost swooned.

Liam didn't have a chance to ask what Graeme was talking about before he felt his hand being grabbed. After a thumb hugging handshake coupled with a chest bump and a hug, Liam watched on as Pauline budged over to welcome Graeme into the cab with a cuddle. Direct and urgent orders were seen being given to the cabbie as he drove off. Liam also started on his way, but with less haste and little else to do.

15

The weather in August can be as temperamental and unpredictable as your grandpa is on Christmas day. On this Indian summer day, Laura's turquoise woollen coat was oppressive as it hung burdensome on her weary shoulders. Trying not to fidget too much, and only occasionally prying her eyes open to gauge what was going on around her, she was being made to wait deliberately. She'd seen it all before, all their dirty little tricks. Onerous uniform apart, she was prepared. She could handle it.

When her name was eventually called, and it was a man's voice, Laura ignored it. When her name was called a second time with a little more urgency, she roused from her simulated slumber to see a clock displaying a time of eleven-eighteen. Her appointment had been set for eleven. Bastards. When grudgingly heaving herself forward onto the edge of the communal seating, she saw the uniformed legs and shiny black shoes of the security guard approaching. At ease boy, I know what I'm doing.

Rolling gingerly across onto her right-hand side, Laura used her left hand to dig her walking cane onto the carpeted floor. With the aid of a loud groan she stood up to edge across to the summoning voice. Her head being bowed to manage each step allowed the added benefit of not having any eye contact with her adversaries. You don't gain points for anything, it's all about them finding excuses to dock points from you. They're trained to mark you down for even the most basic levels of human interaction. Bastards.

Flopping her size eight frame down onto a flimsy four-legged plastic chair with little decorum, the back almost gave way to have her on the floor. What a sight that would have been, to see members of staff rushing over to help her onto her feet and brush down her smelly clothes. It was more difficult for any of them to cop a free grope in here though, small blessings. A side-eyed glance across the desk revealed the sight of a sky-blue tie set against a brilliant white shirt. It was a man she'd have to deal with today. Laura wasn't sexist, not at all, but clichés are clichés for a reason. The women, even the one's in here, are sometimes a little more empathetic. Sometimes.

'Hughes. Laura Hughes. Now it makes sense.'

The confirmation of her name from the other side of the desk, over and above the sound of her personal files being shuffled was delivered with what seemed like a knowing smirk. But it was too early yet for any direct eye contact.

'Hi. So, how are you?' The unseen smirk may have morphed into an amiable smile.

The compulsion to avoid eye contact was still strong, but Laura recognised the voice, and it was killing her. Unable to resist any longer, a brief glance up and across the desk confirmed her worst nightmare. Yeah, yeah, yeah. Spiders, clowns, heights and whatever. Blah, blah, blah. They're nothing. 'Fuuuuu.' Laura wanted to scream out loud but couldn't. An internal scream would have to do, for now.

'You look – I'm going to go for different,' the man smiled even more. He'd leaned in and across the desk to deliver his critique on Laura's apparel, and the soft tone he'd used to deliver it was a strange combination of inquisitive and accusing. Another glimpse up confused the situation even more. His smile had changed to a grin, a knowing grin. 'Like I said,' he began again. 'I'm neither a taxman, or a traffic warden.'

Annoying could now be added to that combination of inquisitive and accusing.

Behind the other side of the desk, the civil-servant facing Laura and charged today with dealing with her claim, was one of the three guys who'd come into her cafe whilst on holiday. It was Liam.

Another internal scream would have to suffice.

'It's not what you think.' It was the beginnings of a flimsy apology as Laura tried to gather her thoughts, but it was all she had. Still though, she avoided eye contact. Old habits do indeed die hard, but it was now involuntarily. 'I mean, it's a little more complicated than- '

'Yeah. I know.'

The response from Liam came as a surprise and threw Laura off kilter. As such, she thought it might be better to let him talk for the time-being. She should hold her peace and not incriminate herself any further. She wasn't a fan of cops and robbers or detective shows and films, but from the few she had seen it was usually the bad guys themselves who always talked themselves into trouble. With a million different things running through her mind, Laura wanted more than anything to run outside and fetch Pauline in for help. Unfortunately, this wasn't really an option. Pauline would have the engine running on the car and be channel hopping between different radio stations to suit her current frame of mind. Motorhead would be replaced by Enya, only to then be substituted again for some Rage Against the Machine. Rather than coming inside this place, she'd speed off with a rubber burning wheelspin to leave Laura to her own devices. Pauline loved Laura, of that there was no doubt. But there are limits to everything.

Before heading out to Tenerife to open their café, Pauline had herself been caught 'signing on' as unemployed when she wasn't. They'd been working in a hotel, as chambermaids, when she'd been rumbled. Pauline suspected someone had grassed her up but didn't have any definitive proof. The fact that just one week before she was caught she'd beaten-up one of the kitchen porters, for harassing Laura, was circumstantial evidence only. At only five-foot-six with a perfectly proportioned size ten frame (size twelve between December and March. For comfort), Pauline was one of the nicest people you could meet. Unless you crossed her. Those incidents combined had hastened their move to Spain and their joint venture in self-employment.

'I can only assume my constant questioning finally pissed of my line manager. To such an extent he'd got bored listening to me. Before I went on annual leave, I was doing back office stuff. But as soon as I came back from holiday – boom – and it's all, "you're needed front of house matey". Funny how things turn out isn't it?'

With Liam still leaning in on the desk and happily babbling away, Laura took the opportunity to try and formulate a feasible escape plan. Preferably one with some dignity. Pauline's story of her own departure came to mind. When confronted she'd put up her hands and said, 'fair cop, you got me.' The lady who'd been questioning her, and most likely expecting a grovelling denial or apology had been so taken aback by her front, she allowed her to defend her actions. Pauline remonstrated that the system was stacked against people like her, 'and you,' she'd told the lady with a pointed finger. How was it that those who run the show to make the laws and set the rules, our members of Parliament who are themselves civil servants, can award themselves huge pay rises whilst claiming, if not scamming, anything and everything they could on their expenses?

'Tell me, when did you last get a decent pay rise?' Pauline had leant across the desk to ask her accuser. 'You are but a pawn my dear,' she'd whispered menacingly. 'And it's a rigged game.'

Pauline stood up from her chair to announce to all and sundry that she wouldn't be signing on anymore. Waving goodbye as she left the office, she bid everyone a fond farewell. Unlike our elected politicians she hadn't been wasting any of the governments money. On the contrary, she'd been putting a little bit of money away every fortnight, for her Spanish adventure.

'Is Pauline here with you?'

It was only after he'd mentioned her friends name that Liam managed to drag Laura away from her thoughts, and she regretted immediately nodding her head. What if they were still after her? What if they were expecting her to pay back the couple of hundred quid she'd scammed? Some of these people take it personally, like it's their own bloody money. Brainwashed idiots. As Liam went on again, albeit in a tranquil tone, Laura got back to her own predicament and thoughts pertaining to them. Pauline's grandiose farewell, as fantastic as it sounded wouldn't work for her. Laura's situation was different. Any thoughts of her standing up from her chair to throw away her walking stick was a non-starter. From a theatrical point of view it would have been amazing to see everyone's reaction when she walked out of the benefits office proclaiming a miracle. She could flash everyone the sign of the cross. 'God bless you, and praise be. God bless you, one and all.' That would certainly match, if not trump Pauline's story. And Pauline would enjoy hearing it too. However, this wasn't the time for competition, and there was more to it.

'What do you know?' Pulling herself away from her outlandish and imaginary exit strategy, Laura regained her composure to quiz Liam on something he'd said earlier. 'You said, yeah I know. What do you know?'

'Well,' started Liam, taken aback by Laura's raised head and sudden attention to detail. 'When I came back from holiday, I was speaking to a mate about you. Not one of the mates there with me. Somebody else, and- '

'You were speaking about me?'

Caught himself now, and bang to rights too, Liam removed his arms from the desk. Sitting back studiously he thought a little more, before grinning and then continuing. 'Yeah. I was talking about you. And the holiday overall,' he chuckled softly. 'Get over yourself.' His smile widened to mirror Laura's. 'Anyway,' he went on again, 'I told this mate about the pub I was in, where you do your stand-up routine,' he leaned in again to whisper. 'Anyway, he told me about this old TV show from years back.'

Any and all thoughts of escape were put to one side, Laura was intrigued. When shuffling herself around to face Liam directly, she did so without much fuss or care for anyone who might have been watching her.

'Yosser Hughes and the Boys from the Blackstuff,' Liam continued. 'And now Laura Hughes! Yoz, from behind the bar. He's your dad, Isn't he?'

'It's a nickname from back in the day, because of our surname. And the TV show.' With her words, Laura's chin lowered softly to rest on the hand that held her cane.

'I thought as much.' With Laura seemingly onside, Liam leant in again to ask. 'What's his actual name?'

'His name's Dan.'

'Fuck-off!' Liam half shouted in shock. Having to first check himself, and then all around, he then went on.

'Always with the comedy. You're not being serious. Are you?'

With her chin stuck fast to her hand a laboured nod of her head with softly closing eyes was all Laura could manage. She knew the character her dad had gotten his nickname from, and the joke, because she knew the TV programme. She'd watched all seven episodes of that series several times. Alongside the great music, movies and working-class folk heroes Yoz had introduced his daughter to, he'd also acquainted her with some of the classic old TV shows.

'So, anyway,' said Liam, as he put down the files he'd been diligently pretending to read. Another glance around the office revealed the coast was clear to speak openly. 'That's what I know.'

'I'm still not sure- '

'I had noticed, on holiday. You sometimes walked with a limp, or a sore leg.'

Dropping her head from her hand and her gaze to the floor, Laura told of the medical condition that confines her dad to a wheelchair. She told Liam this affliction was hereditary, with a twenty-five percent chance of it being passed on. She looked up to tell him that she too carried this defective gene. All the messy details, the reports from hospitals and her GP, they would all be recorded in the extensive file he had in front of him. Laura made a last-ditch attempt to justify what she was doing by stressing that she wouldn't have a retirement like any normal person, so to speak. Lowering her look to the floor once more she also claimed what she was doing was done, in part out of self-preservation. Sitting in a call centre for eight hours a day, on a zero-hours contract and minimum wage would leave her no time for her daily stretching and mobility exercises. She also bemoaned how difficult it would be for her to make it to and from the foodbank, which let's face it would be an inevitable side-effect of her being in work. She concluded by telling how unlucky her family had been overall. Between her and her three brothers, a twenty-five percent chance of this defective gene affecting any of them meant she should have been the only one affected. However, one of her brothers has also been diagnosed as a carrier.

'Sooty?'

Raising her head with a squinted eye and peculiar shape to her mouth made it unclear to know what would be released when it was next opened. Laura put Liam out of his misery, 'you remembered his name?' She relaxed a smile. 'Well, not his actual name.'

'I remember lots of things from that holiday.' Liam's raised eyebrows were put to shame by the glint in his eye and sunlight smile.

'If you call him Sooty to his face, he'll kick your arse. He's a judo champion.' Glancing around the sterile office toward the large windows and the front door reminded Laura where she was. She'd momentarily forgotten about, but now remembered her friend waiting outside. 'He only let's Pauline away with that, and only in private. He's a big softie with her.'

'If I called him Sooty? Now, when would I ever have that opportunity?'

A tandem smile filled the otherwise empty space.

'I haven't seen Graeme since we got back from holiday.' Liam had started but paused again. The lady who'd originally been tasked with interviewing Laura came over to see how things were progressing. With a fake smile Liam assured her everything was going to plan.

'I fucking hate this place,' he leant in to snarl in a whisper, as he watched his colleague walk away. 'Yeah, so anyway. Graeme sent me a message on Facebook. He's decided to take the plunge and make the move over to Spain, permanently. And to Tenerife specifically, to be with Pauline.'

The joy in Laura's eyes meant she needn't say anything to confirm what Liam had already been told.

'I sent him a message back straight away. It was a YouTube link, of The Spice Girls,' Liam paused to congratulate himself with a grin. 'Two become one.'

'I know,' Laura smiled. 'Pauline told me, and I wound her up all day.' Pausing for a moment to release a chuckle, Laura then went on again. 'Anytime she was close enough to hear me, I would sing out the lyrics, If you wannabe my lover. Those are the only Spice Girls lyrics I know. Honest.' Pausing again to lean across the desk herself, and to whisper, Laura summed up with a smirk. 'She was fucking fizzing all day. I had a great time.'

'Damn those bloody Spice Girls,' they chuckled in harmony, before checking to see if anyone had noticed their insolent hilarity. Liam took a second to grasp hold of the fact he'd succeeded in making Laura laugh again. It didn't matter that it had been done remotely, or even that she'd received it second-hand.

'Your Facebook profile, and your photograph. They appear on my page quite regularly now. It's a connection thing, I think. People I know and people you know. It did remind me though, of your intro from your compere. No filming or photographs – for security reasons!'

'Yeah, social-security,' laughed Laura, and she was delighted to see Liam laugh too. In for a penny, in for a pound. 'It's a bit late to be worried about that now,' she continued, before they both chuckled some more.

'I've hovered my cursor over your photo a few times. You know, to friend request you. But-'

'How's your writing stuff coming along?'

'Stuff!' scoffed Liam. 'Cheers. And now you want to know – In here, today?' With his hands in the air as he spun around in his comfortably cushioned chair to highlight where they were, Liam intimated that to discuss his 'stuff' in here might not be appropriate. He blew out his disappointment in a sigh. Liam had convinced himself some of the things he'd witnessed on holiday could have been the sun playing tricks on him. Perhaps even the fault of the retro light system in the Tropicana club, with its blue and yellow lightbulbs. But no. Even here today, in this sterile and artificially lit office. Those eyes, Laura's eyes.

'Yeah, okay. Maybe you can tell me about it another time.'

'So, anyway. On the employment front,' started Liam again, primarily to restore eye contact with Laura, but also to alleviate any fluster over what she'd just said and the possible implications. 'What's Graeme going to do out there, for work?'

'There's loads of work, as long as you're not too fussy.' A teasing smile with a forward motioned nod of her head suggested there weren't too many positions for English speaking civil servants. 'Actually,' she began again in a whisper. 'There's a job going free at Yosser's as we speak,' she finished with a mischievous grin.

'Bar staff?'

Changing hands on the grip of her walking stick to wipe at her mouth and hide her snicker, Laura also took advantage of the opportunity to wipe away a little saliva. She wasn't too fussed about her wayward spittle, but she did then ask Liam not to judge her. Reminding him again of the drag artist compere, Dusty Springclean, Laura told what had become of her. She laughed some more when opening her story by saying she'd been 'banged-up', for armed robbery.

Apologising again after Liam had jumped back in his chair at how callous she could be, Laura told how Dusty was pleased to have finally 'made it'. On the day of her arrest she'd been seen on almost every television channel, not just in Tenerife, but throughout Spain. Her mugshot was everywhere. She was wearing her favourite blonde wig and had ruby red lips, although her running mascara was a bit of a let-down. The television channels delighted in showing the CCTV footage from a petrol station, of Dusty threatening a man with what turned out to be a huge dildo wrapped up in a pair of her own tights. They never revealed who the dildo belonged to. They then went on to show the external CCTV footage from street cameras, to show her running away from the police. It took two burly officers to grapple her to the ground, and then three more to hold her down. 'And when I say running away, you have to picture this,' Laura laughed some more. 'She was wearing a lovely vintage dress. It was only cotton, but it was total bombshell. Jesus, I wish she were my size and I could probably have – oh, sorry. Sorry. Anyway, and behind her, fluttering in the wind was her feather boa. Better yet, she was wearing her best high-heels in a size ten. I mean. She could barely walk in those things, let alone run away from the cops.'

A fitting amount of time was given over to contemplate Dusty's predicament, and to allow Laura and Liam time to compose themselves. This was judged to be when Liam had proposed that Dusty, as an entertainer, would probably fare okay in prison. Regardless what jail she was sent to.

'Actually. I have news too, about Martin.' When he then reclined in his chair, Liam flopped his hand forward.

'Ah, you've probably heard it already. From Pauline, via Graeme obviously.'

'Who's Martin?'

'Martin!' Sitting upright again, and with his eyes lit up, Liam carried on with his news as an exclusive. 'Of course! Martin. You know, thingummybob. Or whatever it was you called him. Thingummy would probably have been one of the nicer things you called him.

'Oh right, thingummy. Or Donald.'

'Well, he's gay.' In his excitement, Liam didn't understand or question the Donald thing. He could ask about that some other time. Maybe. 'Yeah, turns out he's gay. Has been all along.'

'Get the fu – I knew it. We knew. Well thought, that there was something. How'd this all come out? Pardon the pun.'

Reminding Laura of the day in the café when Martin had behaved like a decent human being for a change, it was the same day he'd asked her and Pauline out to club Tropicana. He went on to tell how before then, Martin had been boasting of an upcoming orgy he'd arranged with some Swedish twins. Well. Rather than any illicit debauchery actually occurring, he'd taken himself off to sleep on the beach. Alone. It was all as usual, nothing more than some fictional and pretentious macho bullshit. His cocky and aggressive façade was nothing more than an elaborate cover story all along. Anyway, rather than sleeping alone on the beach that night, some middle-class guitar playing hippy called Sebastian happened upon him. The two of them spent the whole night talking, apparently. Over the next couple of days me and Graeme barely saw him. I guess one thing must have led to another.'

'We do get a lot of those blue-eyed blonde-haired Swedish twins in the café. And they're always horny as hell.' Laura laughed, before then reminding Liam who'd asked whom, regards the night out in Tropicana.

'Yeah, fair enough,' laughed Liam, before going on again, 'In the airport departure lounge when coming home, Martin had barely spoken a word. Then out of the blue he'd said he needed to go and do something urgent. When he came back, it was then he told us about his trysts with this Sebastian bloke, and that he was gay. He said he'd known about it for a while, but felt it best to keep it hidden. The urgent thing he'd needed to do, was to telephone his mum. He'd wanted her to be the first person he told about his sexuality. He'd also been afraid as to how his dad would take the news, although he was fine with it apparently. "About bloody time he came out of that fucking closet," he'd said. Anyway. This Sebastian bloke lives in Colchester, and Martin's been invited down to meet the family.'

'You have to watch out for those middle-class boys though,' Laura's eyes and tilted head displayed a touch of scepticism. 'Some of them just want a hug from their mummy, but they don't know how to ask for it.'

'I know,' Liam agreed. 'But he seemed happy for a change. So, you know.'

'It's only you left now.' Wondering why she would involuntarily blurt out whatever thoughts came into her head at any given time, rather than thinking things through first, Laura was relieved when Liam seemed to find some humour in what she'd said.

'That's right, yeah,' he smiled. He leant across the desk again to whisper, as if he were telling tales about someone behind their back. 'My old granny and her words of wisdom huh? I might have to rethink my approach on that. She thinks she might have worked out a system to beat the National Lottery. On the plus-side,' he giggled. 'Who knows, we might be millionaires soon.'

A glance around the office brought into view the clock on the wall. Although Liam hadn't conducted one of these interviews for a while, he knew they'd already exceeded an appropriate amount of time given over for such things. Laura's eyes had followed Liam's, and she too watched on as the clicking sound of another wistful minute turning over on the mounted clock broke an otherwise sombre silence. Brought back down to earth with a reality thump, Laura again wondered how this was going to play out.

'So anyway, as I was saying when you first sat down.' A blank look in Laura's eyes told Liam she probably hadn't understood much of anything he'd been saying. Her eyes shone so much brighter when she smiled, and he wondered if he'd see anything so vivid again. She was clearly in a state of shock that he'd sprung this surprise on her. He wasn't sorry. He would have done anything, almost anything to have seen her again. But it was time to put her out of her misery and set her free. Maybe.

'As I was saying,' he leant across to whisper with a smile, hoping to put her at ease again. 'I'm done here, with all of this shit I mean. The clocking-in and the clocking-out.' Seeing Laura giggle at this point, although he wasn't sure why, at least assured Liam he had her listening again. 'I've decided to take a leaf out of Graeme's book, to try something different. I've got some savings and I want to try something new. Who knows, and don't laugh, I might take some time out to see if my writing is up to much. Anyway. With regards to yourself and this appointment, my recommendation going forward will be that in my opinion, bringing you in here once a month is - And no offence, a pointless exercise that can only be detrimental to both your physical health and your mental wellbeing.'

Without warning, Liam stood up from his chair and he took Laura's files with him. 'Miss Hughes,' he started, and loud enough for everyone to hear. 'Thank-you so much for your time, and I'm so sorry we had to call you in here today. I will update your file, and my line manager with some of the things we've discussed today. Thank-you and goodbye.'

The clammy feeling that enveloped Laura since she'd put on her uniform had managed to get worse during the earlier parts of this surprise encounter. The chill that now encircled her entire body was a complete contrast, but equally troubling. A quick check to make sure she was fully clothed, she was, brought with it a dizzy spell and a momentary lapse of reason. She hoped to be sick, to rid her body of this horrible and disconcerting state of despondency that was now all consuming. At points throughout this interview she'd imagined how it would end. This option though, this scenario, it hadn't been a consideration. This wasn't how it was supposed to end, this couldn't be the end. When uneasily, though not for the usual reasons, pushing her walking stick onto the floor to lift herself off the chair, Laura didn't know what to say or do. She stared bewildered at Liam who with his head down held her files in his crossed arms and against his chest. Edging herself around and away, Laura couldn't fathom why her legs weren't working as they should. She wasn't playacting, she knew when her bad spells were, and she knew what caused them. But this, now! She couldn't interpret.

Laura was just about managing to hold her balance, her nerves were another matter. She couldn't. No, she wouldn't fall down here.

Staring out at the large windows and the plate glass front doors, Laura saw her path to freedom. There was no-one standing in her way and nothing to hold her back, but she couldn't move.

When Liam looked up to see Laura in some difficulty, he wasn't sure what to do. She could be playing to the crowd, so to speak, and he didn't want to interfere. On the other hand, she might need some help. When Laura turned herself around to face him again, after he'd given in to ask if she needed any help, he was at once enthralled and embraced by those emerald green eyes. They were animated and they sparkled.

'That photograph on Facebook,' Laura started. 'You should listen to your wise old granny. The very next chance you get,' she smiled. 'Click on it. Que sera, sera.'

Thank-you.

@GrossIndecency1

TOTAL

FOOD ORDER
Table 3

2 b'fasts
1 with broken toast
1 no shrooms,
   blah blah blah
   married
2 espressos

Liam – graeme

Coffee – ToGo

By the same author

Gross Indecency

A very British rom-com, with a touch of nostalgia.

In 1967 the British government decriminalised homosexuality.
This story has been fifty years in the making.
The characters and events in this book are based on real stories.
Tens of thousands of them.

Printed in Great Britain
by Amazon

41515468R00104